I0451041

Frozen in Jeopardy

Danger in Destiny
Book 2

Melanie D. Snitker

DALHOUSE MEDIA, LLC

Frozen in Jeopardy
Danger in Destiny: Book 2
By Melanie D. Snitker

Dallionz Media, LLC
P.O. Box 5283
Abilene, TX 79608

Cover Art: Dallionz Media, LLC

Melanie D. Snitker
melanie@melaniedsnitker.com
www.melaniedsnitker.com

This is a work of fiction. Names, characters, businesses, places, events, and incidents either are the products of the author's imagination or used in a fictitious manner. Any resemblance to actual persons, living or dead, or actual events is purely coincidental.

For Loki,
my canine best friend
who did what I thought
was impossible and turned
me into a dog person.
I love you, buds!

Chapter One

Paige Wade stood in front of the glass doors and frowned. To see Destiny, Texas, get snow so early in the season was practically unheard of.

A blanket of white covered the ground and parking lot outside Destiny Animal Hospital. The only reason the pathway was clear was because Paige had found the remnants of an old bag of rock salt in the storage room and sprinkled it from the doors to the parking lot in case anyone needed to get inside.

She'd also sent most of the staff home earlier in the day. Few people in town knew how to drive in inclement weather. Paige included, if she were honest. But she was already at the clinic when the snow started, and she'd rather stay than have to drive back or create a situation where someone else had to drive in.

The only other person who'd remained was Selena Sanchez, one of the talented vet techs who lived less than a block away.

Paige should've insisted Selena go home, too. They hadn't had a single patient come by all day. Now that business hours were over, Paige would lock the doors, and they'd only be opened again in the case of an emergency.

Selena walked up and stood with Paige. They gazed outside together for several moments in silence.

"It's pretty. But I'm glad we only see it a couple times a year." Selena's breath fogged the glass as she spoke. "Trey was going to take me out for breakfast tomorrow morning, but I'm thinking we'll have to reschedule."

Selena and Trey had been dating for several months, and it looked like the relationship was getting serious. Paige had seen Trey a couple times when he swung by the clinic to pick up Selena for lunch.

"That would probably be best. If you can, avoid getting out in this until it all melts."

Selena typed a text message on her phone and sent it. "What about you?" she asked as she pocketed the device.

Paige knew exactly where this was heading. Selena liked to tease her about her lack of a love life and invite Paige to accompany her on social gatherings. Paige always declined, even though she appreciated Selena's efforts. "No plans here. Though I do hope the weather clears before Saturday."

"Oh, that's right. Your friends are getting married. I sure hope it clears up, too."

Paige thought about two of her best friends. Megan Bristow and Bryce Keyes were finally getting married after being reunited last year. When Megan asked Paige to be her maid of honor, it was a no-brainer to agree. The other person in their friend group of four, Gabe Harrison, would stand as Bryce's best man.

Selena tilted her head to one side and glanced at Paige. "Did you find a date to the wedding?"

It took effort for Paige to hide her smile. "No, I don't

have a date to the wedding. I'm going to be busy helping Megan. I'd rather not have to worry about keeping a date company."

"That's okay. I think usually the best man is expected to escort the maid of honor. You'll be fine."

Gabe's handsome face flitted through Paige's mind. The four of them had been friends since school, and it was fitting for them to be in the wedding party together. Now that Bryce and Megan were a couple, it was a little awkward sometimes when it left Paige and Gabe together.

Paige chose not to comment. She was just fine being on her own at the wedding.

"Maybe there'll be something between you and the best man. A wedding isn't the worst place to meet someone." Selena gave her a knowing look.

"The best man is a guy I've known forever who will remain firmly in the friend zone." She patted Selena on the back. "On that note, I'm going to send you home before you put a personals ad in the paper for me. Be careful, okay?"

"I will. Are you heading out?"

Paige had been debating that all afternoon. Destiny Animal Hospital was the only vet clinic in town where a veterinarian was available twenty-four hours a day, seven days a week. Once official office hours were over, the doors remained locked. Most of the time, the vet on call—that was Paige tonight—would go home. If anyone needed their services, Paige and a tech would go back in and tend to the animal as needed. There were days or weeks when things were crazy and extra hours were worked, and others where the vet on call didn't have to go in at night at all.

With this snow, though, Paige wasn't sure whether to make the trip home and hope she didn't have to come back again or go ahead and sleep here at the hospital in case of an overnight emergency, then go home tomorrow.

She was about to tell Selena she would wait a while longer when a gray car flew across the parking lot. Paige braced a hand against the door, fully expecting the car to skid out of control. It turned sharply as it approached the clinic, the tires on the right side jumping the curb before the vehicle jerked to a stop.

Paige unlocked the door and stepped into the frigid air. At least the snow had stopped falling.

A man nearly stumbled out of the driver's side, then used one hand to steady himself as he went around the front of the car. He yanked open the back door nearest the clinic. "Please, help my dog," he called over his shoulder.

Paige turned to Selena, who was standing in the doorway of the clinic. "Get a stretcher."

Selena nodded once and disappeared inside.

Paige carefully jogged down the pathway, the rock salt crunching beneath her shoes.

The man struggled to lift something. He finally turned as Paige neared. Blood smeared the tan, button-down shirt that was only partially tucked into his slacks. "Please, you have to help her. She doesn't deserve this." He staggered to the side, grabbing the open door for support.

Paige slipped past him so she could see inside, aware of the sound of Selena running down the pathway to join them.

The dog, which looked to be primarily an American pit bull terrier, was lying on her side on a large coat. Blood marred her tan and white fur, and a large gash on her side continued to ooze blood. "What happened to her?" Knowing what kind of wound it was would go a long way in helping them know how to treat the dog.

4

Silence answered her question. She turned to find the man with one hand against his side as he leaned into the car door. "Car. Hit by a car."

That meant there was a high probability of internal damage in addition to what she was seeing here. The dog was lying so still, Paige was afraid she'd died in transit. It wasn't until Paige leaned over her that the dog's head turned and large, brown eyes met her own. Fear, pain, and exhaustion were evident, but so was hope.

They needed to get the dog inside. Now.

Paige motioned Selena closer. Together, the women lifted the injured dog and lowered her onto the stretcher. "We'll do our best to help her," Paige promised.

"Thank you," the man said sincerely, tears in his eyes. "I never meant for anything to happen to her."

"Of course." Selena led the way as they carried the stretcher up the path toward the clinic. A door slammed shut behind her. Paige turned, expecting to see the man jogging to catch up to them. Instead, he stumbled his way back to the driver's side. He'd nearly made it before slipping and falling in the snow. "Hold on, Selena." She gently set her side of the stretcher down.

Paige was ready to help the man stand and was relieved when he picked himself up. He slid into the driver's seat of the car. "Wait, sir. I need you to come in and fill out some paperwork. We need your contact information." He closed the door. "What's the dog's name?"

The wheels spun as they fought for traction on the snowy pavement before the car took off again, weaving its way across the parking lot and disappearing into the night.

An ache formed in the back of Paige's throat. Something wasn't right. "Come on, let's get her inside."

They carried the dog back into the warmth of the clinic. Paige made sure the doors clicked and locked behind them.

"It looks bad," Selena said.

"Yeah, it does."

"Why didn't the guy come in with us? That was weird, right?"

"Definitely."

"We're still going to help her, aren't we?" Selena's eyebrows drew together as she looked at the dog who was lying still on the stretcher.

As a rule, they didn't usually bring animals in without someone who was willing to pay for treatment. If they did that too often, then the animal hospital would go out of business. It was something the owner, and fellow veterinarian, Reginald Smith, taught her years ago.

However, there was a fund that people donated to that was used for the occasional case if either Paige or Reg deemed it a dire situation. As far as Paige was concerned, this was one of them.

The pittie wasn't struggling to move, but from the way she kept looking around, it was clear she wondered where her owner was. Paige's heart ached for her. *Guide my hands, God. And please give her the peace and strength she needs to make it through this.*

"We're going to do everything we can to save her life."

Nearly two hours later, Paige yawned as she sagged against a counter. The long, boring day had turned into a medical emergency, and it was catching up with her. The sudden decline in adrenaline led to exhaustion and a stomach aching with hunger.

She reached a hand into the large kennel and ran it lightly over the dog's head. As soon as they'd gotten her inside and started looking at her injuries, it was clear to Paige they were not caused by a vehicle.

In this case, the dog had a bloody nose, some bruising in her mouth, and one deep laceration on her side near her shoulder. Paige couldn't know for sure, but she strongly suspected the dog was involved in a fight with a human. Whether the dog attacked, and the human only defended himself, or it was the dog who had been on the defensive, it was impossible to determine. Either way, the laceration was likely caused by a knife.

Thankfully, the wound wasn't too deep, and Paige was able to stitch it closed. Due to the length of the cut, the dog would need to be watched closely to make sure she didn't pull at the stitches until the wound had enough time to start healing.

With any luck, she'd make a full recovery, even if the jagged scar would always be a visible reminder of the trauma that she had survived.

"You should wear it proudly," Paige whispered. Then she turned her thoughts heavenward. "Thank you, Father, for helping this girl. Thank you that we were able to patch her up. Please give her strength as she heals."

Paige decided to wait until morning, confer with Reg, and then call the police to report the incident. Especially if the dog's owner never returned.

The bright blue collar and leash hanging from the door of the kennel drew Paige's attention. Both appeared brand new. She took a closer look at the lone tag that hung from the collar. It had a phone number on it.

Paige immediately pulled her phone out and dialed the

number. Instead of ringing, it went straight to an automated voicemail box.

"Hello, this is Dr. Paige Wade from Destiny Animal Hospital. I was hoping to give you an update on your dog's condition. Please call me back when you get this." She left her return number and hung up.

Now that the dog's condition was stable, Paige retrieved a scanner and ran it all around the dog's neck, shoulders, and chest, hoping someone had thought to microchip her.

There it was. But when she tried to put the number into their database, it came back with an error. She tried again, but the result was the same. Sometimes owners have their pet microchipped but then never get around to registering them. That was too bad, because Paige hated the idea of the pittie's owner worrying about her.

It was difficult to know how long it would be before the dog started to wake up. Until then, Paige would check her vitals regularly. Regardless, it meant spending the night at the clinic, but that didn't mean Selena had to.

A glance at her watch reminded Paige it was nearly ten o'clock at night.

Selena peeked her head around the corner. "Everything okay with our Jane Dog?"

One corner of Paige's mouth quirked at the nickname the younger woman had given their patient. "She's stable and doing well. Did you have a chance to eat?"

Selena held up the last bite of her sandwich which she promptly popped into her mouth. She gave a thumbs-up.

"Perfect. I need to run out to my car and grab my backpack. I never did bring it inside today. If you could keep an eye on her for a few minutes, you should be clear to head home when I get back."

Selena dusted her hands off, rolled a stool near the large

8

kennel where Jane Dog was resting, her IV tubes running through the grating in the door. "I've got her."

"I'll hurry." Mostly because it was miserably cold outside, and Paige did not look forward to going out in it.

Paige always carried a bag with essentials exactly for nights like this. It held everything from a clean shirt to snack foods. Most of the time, she never had to bring the bag into the building.

She zipped up her coat and tapped a front pocket to make sure she still had her keys before letting herself out the doors. Frigid air hit her face as the doors clicked behind her, locking her out. It was a precaution they took after normal business hours since the veterinarian was often alone, and they stored medications inside.

Paige breathed in the scent of an early winter. At least the wind had died down, leaving everything quiet and peaceful. The only sound was the crunch of rock salt beneath her shoes as she traversed the walkway.

The snow where the walkway met the parking lot was a mess thanks to the car earlier. Spots of blood sprinkled the snow from when they'd eased the dog out of the car. She needed that cleaned up before they opened again in the morning. There was something on the ground near the blood, but she couldn't see well enough to figure out what it was.

She kept a flashlight in her glove compartment and decided to grab that and check it out on the way back.

Once she got to the parking lot, Paige had to pick her way across so as not to slip. She normally parked toward the back to make room for patients, but next time there was weather like this, she'd choose a closer spot or take her bag inside with her just in case.

With any luck, the snow would melt tomorrow.

She reached the far side of the small parking lot where her older car was parked alongside Selena's. She hit the key fob to unlock the door and pulled it open. The poor hinge always creaked like a wounded animal, but here in the dark, the sound seemed to echo all around her.

Paige cringed. She should probably get that fixed. Although, truth be told, it'd take a lot more than fixing the door to improve the car. Megan was always teasing her about trading it in for something new.

Paige covered another yawn as exhaustion flooded her body. She snagged her backpack from the floorboard and flung it over one shoulder. Then she retrieved her flashlight from the glove compartment before locking and closing the car door again with another loud creak.

The lone streetlight standing over the parking lot acted like a sentinel, its yellow-tinged light barely reaching the back of the lot. The protection it offered from the darkness on a Wednesday night waned again near the sidewalk leading to the building. Another light above the animal hospital's entrance took up duty on the other side. The lights seemed brighter than normal as the snow on the ground reflected the glow.

Paige breathed deeply, the cold air stinging her lungs. What she needed was a strong cup of coffee, a fresh shirt, and maybe a sandwich.

She walked back to the blood splatter, turned her flashlight on to get a better look, and gasped.

Blood smeared the snow and pooled in the bottom of a shoe-shaped impression where the guy had fallen before getting back in his car. She panned her flashlight around the area, noting the drops of blood that splattered the snow around where the car used to be.

The dog hadn't been the only one in that car who was injured.

The hair on the back of her neck rose as something drew her attention to the front of the clinic.

She couldn't quite pinpoint the source of the sound. Silence filled the air around her.

A quick scan of the parking lot revealed nothing, but a sense of urgency flared in her chest.

She shoved her flashlight back into her pocket and withdrew her keys so that she was prepared to get back into the building. The fact that the door remained locked made her feel more secure when she did stay overnight. Right now, though, it seemed more like a barrier between herself and safety.

Silence.

Too much silence.

Just when she thought her mind was playing tricks on her, there was no denying the shuffling sound to her left as a figure dashed from the shadows and headed toward her.

With the keys in one hand and the other gripping the backpack strap, Paige dashed for the building. Puffs of warm air exploded from her mouth in clouds. Heavier footfalls pounded the snow-covered pavement behind her.

Terror splashed over her like ice water.

Paige spared a quick glance behind her long enough to register the black figure chasing after her. There's no way she would reach the doors before her pursuer caught up.

She swallowed her panic, made herself breathe, and kept her focus on the doors ahead of her. As soon as her feet hit the walkway, she spun around. In the same motion, she jerked her backpack off her shoulder.

The guy—he was clearly a man now that she was facing him—kept running at her, closing the distance between them much faster than she thought he would. Her heart stalled.

With a key extended between her fingers like a blade, she punched at him with her fist. The key grazed his hand as he grabbed for her arm. Every part of his body was covered with black fabric from the gloves on his hand to the balaclava over his face. He probably didn't even feel the key's impact.

With one hand wrapped around her wrist, he used the other to try and wrench the keys from her grasp. He held so tightly that her wrist screamed in agony.

Paige flung her other arm wide and brought it around with as much force as she could muster. The backpack struck her assailant on the side of his face.

It must have shocked him because his eyes—the only part of him that wasn't covered—shifted to look directly at her. The pupils dilated, and Paige noted startling blue irises.

His grip loosened enough for her to slip free. She hit the panic button on her key fob. Her car sprang to life as the alarm sounded and lights flashed.

Without hesitation, Paige ran to the entrance of the clinic. By the time she got there, Selena was looking through the doors with wide eyes.

"Call 9-1-1!" Paige commanded with a slap of her hand against the glass.

Selena nodded and started jabbing at her cell phone.

Paige looked behind her again, fully expecting her attacker to be lunging at her. Instead, only cold air, the car alarm, and the sound of her own quick breaths greeted her.

Chapter Two

Police Officer Gabe Harrison steered his department-issued Tahoe through the quiet streets of Destiny. With only an hour left in his shift, he was looking forward to going home and getting some rest. The snow they'd gotten today—up to five inches in some areas—had been enough to create havoc on the roads. Especially now that temperatures had dropped, and some roads were quickly freezing over.

He'd lost count of how many accidents or disabled vehicles he'd assisted with.

One thing was certain: Destiny was not prepared for winter weather.

Gabe was perfectly fine with the fact that they got little winter precipitation most years. As far as he was concerned, it was a huge checkmark in the plus column when it came to living in this area of Texas.

The sound of Loki, his K-9 partner, yawning in the back had Gabe nodding his agreement. "I hear you, buddy. I think we've more than earned some sleep tonight."

For most of the calls today, the German shepherd had

stayed in the heated Tahoe. Unlike Gabe, whose feet felt frozen to the core. How long would it take to thaw his toes out once he got home and into some dry socks? He looked forward to finding out.

He'd patrol another half hour then head back to the Destiny Police Department to check in before calling it a night.

The radio came to life as dispatch announced a report coming in from the Destiny Animal Hospital, including an abandoned animal, possible stabbing, and an attempted assault.

Gabe was instantly on alert. Paige, one of his close friends, worked there. He had no idea if she was in the building now, but the possibility that she might be and hearing the words "stabbing" and "assault" brought up images he forcibly shoved aside. The clinic was across town, but there was no way he wasn't heading there to make sure Paige was okay.

By the time he arrived, three other police cars were already there. Gabe immediately recognized Paige's car at the back of the lot. He parked the Tahoe close to the front of the building, left Loki in his kennel, and jogged to the group of officers.

Their flashlights illuminated blood all over the snow, and Gabe's heart plummeted. "What happened?"

Officer Clint Baker shook his hand. "Hey, Harrison. You know Dr. Wade, right?"

"I do. Is she okay?"

"She's fine. Paris is inside getting her statement."

Thank God. Gabe pointed to the mess on the snow. "So whose blood is this?"

"According to Dr. Wade, this guy came roaring into the

parking lot, said his dog needed help, and asked her to save it. Before Dr. Wade could even get the dog inside, the guy tripped on the way back to his car and took off like a crazy man." Baker pointed to the largest blood spot on the ground. "She said this is where he tripped. We tested it, and it's human."

Gabe tried to grasp what Baker was telling him. "The man was injured, too."

"Looks like it. The doc says the dog was likely cut with a knife or something similar. It could be the owner was, too. She said she noticed him holding his side and leaning against the car door." Baker motioned to the front of the building. "We're still trying to determine whether the guy who attacked her is related to this case."

Paige was attacked?

Gabe turned and jogged up the pathway. A woman in blue scrubs with brown paw prints all over them saw him approach and opened the doors. He immediately zeroed in on Paige leaning against the check-in counter as she spoke to Detective John Paris.

The moment she spotted Gabe, she pushed away from the counter and strode toward him. "Hey. Thanks for coming." She slipped her arms around him.

He held her close. He'd known Paige since middle school, and she wasn't a hugger. The only other time she'd ever hugged him had been at her brother's funeral. "What happened? Are you okay?"

"Yeah." She stepped away and gestured toward the door. "I went to get a bag out of my car and some guy chased me. Grabbed my arm."

She held her right hand out. He took it in his and turned it over. A light bruise was forming across the soft skin of her wrist. That anything worse might have happened to her had him clenching his jaw. "Did he say anything?"

"No." She crossed her arms in front of her body. "But it seemed like he was trying to get the keys out of my hand. Maybe he was hoping to get inside and gain access to the pain medications we keep in stock. It wouldn't be the first time."

It's true that drug addicts will find their fix wherever they can. While the animal clinic only kept pain medication to be used for animals, it wasn't all that different from what was prescribed to help humans.

"Maybe. But it seems like a huge coincidence given the other excitement you've been dealing with tonight."

Paige looked at her watch, then turned to address the woman who let him in earlier. "Selena, will you please do a stat check on Jane Dog?"

"Of course." With a nod, the tech left the room.

Detective Paris stepped forward. "Hey, Harrison. Dr. Wade said that the attack happened out in front of the building. He chased her partway up the walkway outside. A combination of activating her car alarm and hitting him with her backpack seemed to scare him off. We haven't canvassed the area yet. We saw a set of footprints in the snow going across the front of the building. But if the perp goes to an area with higher traffic, we may need Loki to work his magic."

Loki was well known in the department for his ability to track a suspect. He held two national certifications show-casing his skills. If the guy who attacked Paige was still around, Gabe had every intention of finding him. "You got it."

He turned his attention to Paige. She was completely in control of most situations. Even now, she seemed to be fine.

But he knew her well enough to spot the way she kept fiddling with the hem of her scrubs and how she took a deep breath before responding to Paris's questions. She wasn't acting herself. After everything that happened, she had to be shaken. "Are you going to be okay?"

"I'll be fine."

Gabe knew she would respond that way no matter how she felt.

"I'll finish taking her statement," Paris said.

Gabe reached out and cupped her elbow with his hand. "I'll be back to check on you when we finish our search," he promised.

She only nodded her understanding, but he didn't miss the flash of relief in her eyes.

Once outside, he checked in with dispatch about the search and then proceeded to get Loki ready. Gabe put a flat collar around the dog's neck, attached a long leash that would allow the dog as much freedom to track as possible, and pocketed the rope toy that Loki loved. "Come on, boy."

Two officers joined them, staying behind the man and dog team to cover their backs. Since they knew where the attacker had come from, Gabe led Loki there so he could pick up the scent and then gave him the command.

Gabe noted the footprints led to the path in front of the clinic, then came back and went the opposite way. He could steer Loki that way knowing it was the direction the perpetrator had gone, but he much preferred to let the dog lead the way.

A moment or two later, Loki focused on the scent and followed the footprints. Gabe nodded approvingly but held any vocal praise for the end of the search.

Loki followed the scent to the edge of the property,

through some bushes, and to a side street that was mostly clear of snow. The footprints disappeared there as well.

The dog circled the area several times but became disinterested.

One of the officers gestured toward a small puddle of water that hadn't frozen yet. "Another vehicle was waiting here."

"Looks like it." Had the car simply been parked and waiting? Or had someone else been behind the wheel? Gabe withdrew the rope toy. "Good boy, Loki. Good boy." He played tug for a moment before relinquishing the rope to the dog. Gabe glanced around them. "Not much for security cameras out here, either."

Maybe there would be one in front of the clinic. With any luck, it might have caught an image of the man who attacked Paige.

The security footage from the camera in front of the building was no help. Like Paige had reported, any image captured of her assailant showed a man approximately six feet tall entirely clad in black. In fact, the only real detail they had was his eye color. Gabe admired her ability to keep her cool during the attack long enough to take in that detail. It may not be much now, but it was better than nothing.

Footage of the incident earlier wasn't much better. Not only did the man who dropped his dog off never get remotely close enough to get a good image of his face, but it was impossible to see the license plate. At least they were able to get the make and model of the car.

They would have to go off the physical descriptions that Paige and Selena gave them.

Gabe glanced at Paige who was talking to someone on the phone. He could only hear bits and pieces of the conversation, but it sounded like she was talking to the owner of the clinic.

"I'll put a call into the hospitals tonight. Make sure that, if anyone matching the description comes in looking for treatment, someone will notify us," said Paris. "I'll contact all of the emergency clinics as well."

"If he was injured as badly as it sounds like he was, he may not make it to a hospital or clinic."

"We'll put out a BOLO for a gray car that may be parked illegally or seem abandoned."

If the guy drove through town as erratically as he'd driven in the parking lot, a BOLO—be on the lookout—may turn up something.

Paige hung up and slipped her phone into a pocket.

Dispatch chatter came over their radios, and Paris put his notebook away. He turned to Paige. "We appreciate your help, Dr. Wade. I've got your contact number. Please let us know if you hear from the dog's owner or if he returns. We'll let you know if we're able to find him as well." He paused. "I'm curious. What'll happen to the dog if he never shows up?"

"We'll keep her here for a couple of days. After that, she'll require care for a week to ten days to make sure the wound heals properly. Our local animal rescue has foster homes that might take her in until she's ready to be adopted."

"All right." Paris held out a hand to shake hers. "It was good to meet you. You take care."

"I appreciate it. Same goes to you." Paige motioned to the tech standing nearby. "Selena was going to head home.

She's only a block away. Could you follow her to make sure she gets there and inside okay?"

"Absolutely." Paris smiled.

Selena quickly retrieved her things. She glanced at Gabe and gave Paige a knowing look before offering a hug. "He's the best man, isn't he?"

The question might have been meant for Paige alone, but Gabe caught it anyway.

Paige's gaze jumped to his, and her cheeks turned pink. "Mm-hmm. Now go home and get some sleep. Seriously, though, thank you for all your help. I couldn't have done it without you."

"Be careful," Selena told her. She spared another quick glance at Gabe before preceding Paris into the parking lot.

Gabe waited to make sure the door locked behind them before turning to Paige. "Are you staying until business hours start up?"

"That was Reg on the phone. He's coming in to relieve me. We've got a critical patient, so someone needs to stay and keep an eye on her vitals, but he doesn't want me here alone in case the guy comes back."

Gabe had met the older man several times since this was where he brought Loki for health checks and vaccinations. He seemed like a nice guy, but Gabe respected him even more now. He was thinking along the same lines and was also glad she wasn't going to be here alone for the rest of the night.

She covered a yawn.

Gabe pointed to Loki who was snoozing quietly on the floor in one corner of the waiting room. "At least someone's getting some sleep."

Paige laughed, the soft sound filling the empty room. She pulled her long, dark hair over one shoulder. She'd dyed her hair numerous shades through the years but this—her natural color—was his favorite. Blonde highlights shone under the lights overhead.

"I should go check on Jane Dog while I'm waiting for Reg." She smiled. "Selena named her since we didn't have her ID." She motioned for him to follow her to the back. "Poor thing is starting to wake up, but she seems sad."

The moment Gabe moved to follow her, Loki was on his feet and at his side. "Can Loki come with me?"

"Sure, but maybe have him sit at the doorway. I'm not sure how our patient is with other dogs." Paige led the way into a surgical room at the back of the building.

Gabe did as she suggested, instructing Loki to sit and wait. The air was heavy with the smell of antiseptic and noticeably cooler than the waiting room. A large, double-doored cage rested against the wall on one side.

Paige sat on the stool next to the cage and reached for the clipboard hanging on the front. "Her condition is stable, but I think whatever happened to her and her owner was pretty traumatizing."

He knelt beside Paige and peered through the grating of the cage door. An IV line led from the pump to a foreleg. It was easy to see the dog was a pit bull, and a pretty one at that. Tan fur was broken by swirls of white. But Paige was right. The dog kept her chin on her paws, a hopeless look in her eyes. It was nearly enough to break his heart. The only time any interest sparked was when she looked at Paige. "Do you think she'll make a full recovery?"

"Yes, I think she will. The bruising in her mouth will heal quickly. The knife wound will take longer." Paige opened the door and reached in to run a hand over the dog's head. "I think she was after someone, and they either punched or kicked her in the nose and mouth." Jane Dog turned her head enough to gently lick Paige's hand. "Then, when she kept coming, they fought her off with a knife." She slipped her hand beneath the dog's chin and rubbed it. "The question is: Who was defending themselves? The person or the dog?"

"If her owner was injured as well, maybe she was trying to protect him." The dog certainly didn't seem to be dangerous. At least not right now, anyway.

"I'm inclined to agree with you. I sure wish she could tell us her side of the story."

The injured dog shifted around a little before lying back down with a pitiful groan. Paige spoke to her softly. "Take it easy, girl. See, I'm still here."

He watched as she tended to her patient. Paige adjusted the IV, took the dog's temperature, and wrote everything down on the clipboard. Through it all, the dog never took her eyes off Paige's face. "I think you have a fan there."

Paige looked up from the clipboard and smiled into the dog's eyes. "The feeling is mutual. She has a lot of determination in her. Don't you, sweet girl?" She rubbed the dog's nose until the animal drifted off to sleep again. "I hope you guys find her owner, and that he's okay."

Gabe watched her, the kindness she showed the dog made him all the prouder to know her. "Yeah. I hope so, too." Even back in high school, Paige had always had a heart for the underdogs—whether animal or people. Sometimes he wondered if that was why they'd become friends in the first place.

Back then, Gabe was a goofball. On the surface, he had a ton of friends and knew everyone. In reality, he cracked jokes because it made people laugh. But it also meant he used that as a defense mechanism, rarely getting to know other kids enough to have true friends. That is, until Paige invited him to sit with her and her friends at lunch. Before he knew it, he was part of a group of people that looked out for each other.

They still did.

It was hard to believe that Bryce and Megan were finally getting married. Gabe had been happy to accept the part of best man, and he couldn't imagine Megan choosing anyone else but Paige for her maid of honor.

"Are you ready for the wedding?" he asked.

Paige closed the kennel door. "I think so." She tried to step away from the kennel, but her shoe caught on the stool nearby.

Gabe quickly reached out to steady her. As he'd done for years, he ignored the way a simple touch of her hand made him wish things could be different between them.

"Thank you," she said, then nudged the rolling stool further away from them. "I feel like I should be doing more for Megan, you know?"

"You're her best friend and maid of honor. I think that's a lot."

"I appreciate that. It's just that Megan is having such a nice, simple wedding. I don't even have that much to do as her maid of honor. Instead of arranging a bachelorette party or something, we're getting together to watch a movie tomorrow night."

Their friends had decided against separate parties. Instead, they wanted to invite friends and family over to their new place in the spring for an old-fashioned barbecue.

"And I can't think of a better way for you gals to spend time together. It's probably exactly what she needs. Something low-key where she can relax and laugh and have fun."

"You think so?" When he nodded, she smiled. "Thanks. Seriously, though. If I ever get married, I'm going to take a page out of her handbook. The less stress the better."

He couldn't agree more. With his thirtieth birthday coming up later in the year, he was starting to wonder whether marriage was even in the cards for him. Not that he was getting old. But his job was a lot, and he recognized that.

Plus, there was the little issue of having feelings for one of his best friends.

A beautiful best friend who vowed her senior year that she'd never fall for or marry someone in the military or police force.

Paige's declaration had been a heavy blow considering he'd grown up dreaming of becoming a K-9 officer. So Gabe respected her choice. Even understood it, given she'd lost two close family members in the line of duty.

He'd always figured she'd marry someone with a less dangerous career. She dated plenty, but none of the guys seemed to stick. Just the thought of her marrying another man someday was a punch to the chest. His heart felt bruised at the idea.

"I'm glad they went with a small wedding, too. Though I think Bryce would've been happy no matter what she wanted to do."

"No doubt." A smile lifted the corners of her mouth and brightened her tired eyes. "It's fun to see them together, especially after all those years."

The couple had been high school sweethearts. Only when Megan returned to Destiny after the death of her father did she and Bryce reconnect again. Ironically, their firefighter friend had pulled her out of a burning building, which had been the first time they'd seen each other in years.

Gabe took it as proof that often God has a plan in place, even if His children mess things up along the way.

"Are you nervous about being the best man?"

"Not really. As long as I don't lose the wedding ring, I should be golden." He paused. "I take it you are nervous?"

"Maybe a little. It's more the fact that I haven't worn a dress or fancy shoes in years. I tried to convince Megan that jeans are the new wedding trend. She didn't go for it." She gave an exaggerated shrug. "I'm praying I make it down the aisle without tripping over the dress or shoes."

Paige had always been one of the most practical women he knew. She hadn't even worn a dress to their high school graduation.

"I'll pray the same."

She chuckled then. "I appreciate it."

His radio sounded, reminding him that his shift was over a half hour ago. As much as he wanted to stay with Paige until Reg arrived, he needed to get back to the station. By the time he was done checking in there, she'd hopefully be home again and getting some sleep.

As though Paige could read his mind, she tossed him a knowing look. "I'm fine, Gabe. You should go."

Loki lifted his head and stared at Gabe as though he were in favor of that idea. Gabe patted his leg, and the dog stretched before standing by his side.

"Don't open that door for anyone except Reg, okay?"

"Oh, you don't have to worry about that."

"Call me if anything else comes up."

"I will." She reached over and scratched Loki's ear. "Thanks for coming. You didn't have to do that."

"Yeah, I did. Take care of yourself, Paige. I'll see you Saturday."

"See you then." She flashed him a tired smile.

Reluctantly, Gabe led Loki out of the animal hospital, made sure the door locked behind him, and got Loki settled inside the Tahoe.

As he backed out of the parking spot, he looked up to find Paige watching him from the door, her hand raised in farewell.

Gabe couldn't stop thinking about the dog and her owner. Whatever happened, some kind of altercation was involved. He didn't like it that, for one reason or another, violence had landed on Paige's doorstep.

Chapter Three

It wasn't long after Gabe left until Reg arrived, but to Paige, it seemed like hours. She had to make herself not stare out the front door. Part of her wanted to stand watch and make sure no one approached without her knowing about it. Then a flash of the man's covered face and his blue eyes came to mind, and Paige shivered. The idea that he might approach the clinic again was more than a little scary. She would never admit it to anyone else, but when the heater kicked on earlier, Paige jolted at the sound.

When she wasn't thinking about that, she kept replaying the way the first guy dropped Jane Dog off and how he had leaned against his car. How he hadn't been able to get his own dog out of the car. If she'd only realized it, she could have at least insisted on trying to get him some help, too.

Instead of remaining out front, Paige focused on Jane Dog. She made sure all information was in her chart so that Reg would have no trouble continuing her care. She hated having to leave the dog after seeing her through the surgery.

However, at this point, she desperately needed a shower, a warm meal, and some sleep.

Reg called to let her know he'd arrived in the parking lot. She welcomed a hug from the older man and reassured him that she was okay.

"In all my years in this business, this is definitely a first," he said. "I'm going to see about installing some extra lighting and another security camera or two. Chances are we'll never need them, but I'd rather be safe than sorry." He asked her to brief him on their patient before sending her home. "I've got this. Go get some well-deserved rest."

Paige smiled at him. He'd welcomed her into the practice right out of college and had given her the opportunity to prove herself. She couldn't imagine working anywhere else.

"Thanks, Reg. I'll be by later in the afternoon to check on the dog. Will you call me if her condition changes dramatically?"

Reg promised he would, and then watched from the door until she was secure in her car. With a wave to him, she started the engine and began the drive home.

She'd been renting the little 800-square-foot home on Hawthorn Street for nearly five years now. It wasn't exactly what she'd consider her dream home, but it had a nice fenced-in backyard that her dog, Pepper, had loved.

Thinking about the Catahoula she'd raised from a puppy brought tears to Paige's eyes. Sweet Pepper passed away nearly a year ago. The old girl had fallen asleep one night and never awakened. It was the way she would've wanted her doggy friend to go, but it'd broken Paige's heart all the same.

Now that empty yard made her sad whenever she stood outside and pictured the way Pepper ran happy circles through the grass with a tennis ball in her mouth.

Sleep deprivation collided with the stress, and tears slid down her cheeks. She sniffed and swiped at them with annoyance.

Her thoughts shifted to Jane Dog. Was her owner somewhere out there, hurt and worried about her? The fact that he'd made a point of dropping her off at the clinic ought to say something about how much he cared about her.

A traffic light turned red a couple blocks from the clinic. Paige eased to a stop and then grunted when she noticed the car behind her was much too close for comfort. She looked in the rearview mirror but, thanks to the glare of the traffic and streetlights, she couldn't see the driver through the glass.

The light turned green. Paige continued until she turned right to get up on the loop. The car behind her did the same. With any luck, the driver would take one of the several exits between where they were now and the Hawthorn Street exit.

She changed lanes, and the car behind her immediately did the same. When she changed lanes again to test the response, the car followed suit.

Chills danced down her spine. Was she being followed? Was it the same guy who'd tried to hurt her at the clinic? Her wrist ached in response to the thought.

"You're overreacting, Paige. You probably cut the guy off, and he's the type who carries a grudge."

Paige looked at the rearview mirror, then tapped lightly on the brake pedal. If she could catch the license plate number... A license plate holder sporting the Bristow Ford and Dodge dealership logo was in its place.

Instead of taking the Hawthorn Street exit, she zipped over and took the exit before it. As expected, the dark car behind her copied her movements. The last thing she wanted to do was lead this creep right to her house.

She turned into the parking lot of a neighborhood market and wound her way up and down several aisles before pulling up to the curb right outside the store. The market was open twenty-four hours, but few cars were parked. Still, hopefully being right in front of the large windows and sliding glass door would be enough to deter someone from actually making a move.

The dark car meandered through the parking lot, stopped at the other side, then turned onto the street and disappeared.

Paige released a lungful of air. There's no way she'd imagined that whole thing. What were the odds that it would follow her to the loop, all the way here, only to leave before going into the market?

Sleep-induced cobwebs made her doubt herself. Still, she waited another ten minutes. When there was no sign of the car returning, she drove the rest of the way home.

She parked in the broken driveway and wished she had a garage to pull into.

If only she had been able to get a license plate number. Or at least get a glimpse of the person driving the car. She happened to know a police officer who might run the plates if she'd had them.

Thinking about Gabe brought a measure of comfort as she unlocked the door and went inside. She slid the dead-bolt in place before kicking her shoes off and making a beeline for the kitchen.

Tonight's events had shaken her far worse than she'd like to admit. She trusted the other officers working the case. But having Gabe show up made her feel even better. She'd known Gabe longer than most people. She had no doubt he was there for *her*.

She tried to shake off the warm feeling that coiled around her heart.

He was her friend. A dear friend, but *just* her friend.

It was a decision *she'd* made years ago when she chose to avoid relationships with anyone in the military or police.

There was no point in entertaining what-ifs.

With a frown, she prepared a bowl of instant oatmeal, then went to take a shower. By the time the hot water was falling over her shoulders, Paige could have easily curled up on the floor right there and gone to sleep. She finished washing her hair, stepped out, and put on her favorite pair of warm pajamas.

The only thing she needed was a glass of water and then she could go and get some sleep.

With her phone in one hand, she snatched the empty glass off her side table with the other and went to the kitchen to pour some cold water from a pitcher in the fridge.

She'd just picked up the glass of water when her phone rang. She recognized the number from Jane Dog's tag and answered it quickly. Maybe her owner was okay and wanted an update on her.

"Hello, this is Dr. Wade."

Several seconds of silence, punctuated by the sound of someone breathing in the background, gave Paige the creeps.

"Who is this?"

An intense feeling of being watched hit her. She balanced the phone between her ear and shoulder. With her free hand, she pulled one of the window blind slats down so she could look out at the front yard.

A dark-colored car sat parked next to the curb. It hadn't

been there when she got home. It was too dark to see well, but she could make out the shape of a person staring at her house. She hung up the phone, then watched in horror as the figure lowered a phone from his ear. A moment later, the car pulled away and sped down the street.

The glass slipped out of Paige's hand and landed on the floor, glass shards and water going everywhere.

"I feel like an idiot." Paige groaned as she ushered Gabe into her house. "I get that I'm jumpy after everything at work, but I *know* that car followed me across town. And why would there be someone sitting outside my house at this time of the night?" It was nearly one in the morning now. "Maybe it was a coincidence that he got off the phone at the same time I did. Or what if that wasn't a phone at all?" She couldn't stop second-guessing herself. Her relief was huge when she saw Gabe and Loki pull into the driveway behind her car.

Calling him for help had been her first reaction. At least she knew he wouldn't hesitate to tell her if he thought she was overreacting.

"You've got great instincts, Paige. I believe you. We're going to get to the bottom of this." He reached for her phone and hit redial but hung up seconds later. "The phone's been turned off." His gaze swept over the combined living room, dining room, and kitchen space and then stopped at the broken glass and water on the linoleum floor.

He escorted Loki to the other side of the room and told him to stay. "Are you okay?" He pointed to her feet.

Only then did she realize she'd been cut earlier by one of the shards. A thin trail of blood led from the top of a big toe and down the side of her foot. "Oh! Yeah, the car startled me, and I dropped my glass." She shifted her foot. "I didn't realize I cut myself, though."

"Come on. Sit down for a minute." He led her to the table and pulled a chair out for her. "Where is your broom?"

"Next to the washing machine in the utility room."

With a nod, he retrieved the broom, a dustpan, and a mop. Within minutes, he'd swept up the glass and mopped the rest of the standing water. "Were you able to tell anything about the car that was following you?"

"It was some type of sedan." She closed her eyes and replayed the drive home in her mind. "There was a Toyota emblem on the front. The car was either a dark blue or black, it was hard to tell." When she opened her eyes, she found Gabe watching her with approval.

"Good job. Did you see any part of the license plate?" He leaned the mop against the counter.

"There was no actual license plate. There was one of those dealership plates instead. Bristow Ford and Dodge."

Gabe seemed impressed. "That alone could be a huge help, especially if they recently purchased the vehicle from there. Now, for the car that was parked out front. Are you certain it was the same car that followed you?"

"Honestly? No, I can't be sure. I never saw the license plates—or lack thereof—for the car out front. But it was the same style and color as the first one. Besides, why would it speed off as soon as the driver realized I spotted him?"

"I'm not doubting you, Paige. In fact, you were calm after everything that happened at the clinic. I have a hard time believing that you'd flip out now over nothing." He motioned to her foot. "Where's your first aid kit?"

"I don't need it." When he gave her that determined look of his, she knew he wasn't going to let it go. "It's underneath the bathroom counter on the right side." She was too tired to argue over it.

When Gabe got back, he set the first aid kit on the table and opened it. He withdrew an alcohol wipe and bandage, then sat in a chair near her. "Here, let me see it."

"I'm fine." Paige held her foot out anyway because she knew he wouldn't relent until she did.

He cupped her heel before lowering her leg across his knee. "As a vet you know well that even the smallest wound can become infected if you don't take care of it." He opened the alcohol swab and carefully wiped away the dried blood before cleaning the tiny cut. "Are you telling me that vets, like doctors, are terrible patients?" There was humor in the twitch of his lips as he glanced at her.

"I'm a terrible patient—it has nothing to do with being a vet."

Gabe chuckled. "At least you're being truthful." He opened a bandage and applied some antibiotic cream to the pad. "Do you remember when you broke your leg in eighth grade? There you were, struggling to go up the stairs on crutches, and you refused help."

"I didn't need help." Paige crossed her arms in front of her. "You were impatient."

"No." He gently placed the bandage over the wound. "The second bell went off, and we were going to be late to class." After pressing the adhesive ends to make sure they would stay, he rested his hand on her foot.

She tried to ignore the way his touch made her skin warm. The entire situation felt way too intimate. "You didn't have to be late for class. You could have gone on ahead."

"I wasn't going to leave you." He paused then, the weight of his words resting in the space between them. "You have no idea how tempted I was to pick you up and carry you to the top of the stairs. I knew you'd never forgive me if I did, so I walked with you instead."

"You're right. I would've been mortified."

"You're stubborn." He ran the nail of one finger across the bottom of her foot.

She jerked it away from him and set it back on the floor. "As if you aren't."

Megan enjoyed pointing out how alike the two of them were, something they both denied.

It looked like Gabe was going to say something else. Instead, he gathered up the pieces of trash and closed the first aid kit. When he got up to throw the trash away, Loki came over. Gabe scratched the dog behind the ears, then looked at Paige. "Have you gotten any sleep?"

"Not yet." She took in his jeans and long-sleeved pullover shirt. He'd probably just gotten home and was trying to sleep himself when she called. "I woke you up, didn't I?"

"Don't worry about it." He flashed her one of those grins that always seemed to put people at ease before sitting back down again. Or, in Paige's case, made her heart flutter even when she didn't want it to. The stubble on his face gave him a rugged look she didn't often see. It was a realization she quickly tried to ignore.

"So why is he tailing me? It doesn't make a lot of sense."

Gabe seemed to be going through scenarios in his mind. "If it is the guy who came after you at the clinic, maybe you hurt him more than you thought you did."

"And it made him angry, so he thought he'd follow me and see if there was an opportunity for payback." Paige cringed. "Too bad I didn't hit him harder, then."

Gabe chuckled with a shake of his head. "He's lucky he

wasn't carrying a kickball, or he might not have made it at all." His brown eyes glittered with amusement.

"Oh, hush." She shoved his leg good-naturedly as heat traveled up her neck and into her cheeks. Back in gym class in junior high, she'd gone to kick the ball only to miss and hit Gabe right in the crotch. He hadn't been seriously injured, but he never let her forget it.

Gabe sobered. "The fact is, they had what we presume is the dog's owner's phone. I think it's safe to say that they are involved somehow."

"Fabulous."

He ran a hand through his thick, black hair that always seemed to be slightly disheveled. How many times had she wanted to reach out and smooth it back into place?

A yawn took over, causing her eyes to water. "Gabe?"

"Yeah?"

"Can you stay for a little while?"

"Of course." He waited for her to stand up before getting her a fresh glass of cold water. "Go get some rest. I'll camp out on the couch. I'll sleep better here anyway knowing that you're okay. Tomorrow, we'll go by the department to see if they've found out anything else about the attack."

"Let me grab you a pillow and blanket."

"Just tell me where they are, and I'll get them."

She pointed to a small hall closet, then accepted the drink and took a sip. She was going to ask if he was sure, but the determination on his face told her all she needed to know. "Thanks, Gabe."

He only gave her a small nod. She went into her bedroom and shut her door then hesitated a moment before setting her glass on the side table and climbing into bed.

As tired as she was, she should've been able to fall

asleep immediately. Instead, she kept picturing the bloody snow and a pair of bright blue eyes staring at her.

She finally focused her attention on Gabe. She pictured him in the living room, sitting on the couch, and keeping an eye on the place.

"Thank you, God, for keeping me safe. For sending help. But most of all, thank you for the kind of friend who'll drop everything to be here when I need him most."

Peace flowed from her head to her toes. The last thing that went through her mind before sleep claimed her was the sound of Gabe's laughter and the smile on his face.

Chapter Four

G abe gave up trying to sleep around six in the morning and sat up with a groan. Paige's couch was horrible. It was lumpy in some spots and thin in others. Not much in between. He probably would've been better off trying to sleep on the floor with Loki. The whole time he kept trying to rest, he couldn't stop listening for the sound of an engine out front. He even checked multiple times to see if there was any activity, but the dark car never did return.

Assuming the person driving the car had been following Paige, hopefully seeing a police vehicle in the driveway would act as some kind of deterrent. In fact, he had every intention of patrolling the area tonight when he was back on duty. He wanted to make it clear that, even though Paige lived alone, she was anything but.

That Paige asked him to stay was a testament to how much everything had freaked her out.

Gabe spent time checking e-mail on his phone and browsing the news. At seven, an alarm sounded from Paige's room, and he heard her stir. He went to her kitchen and started looking around to see what was available for break-fast. The only coffee in the house was a jar of instant. He couldn't wait to tease her about it.

It didn't take long for her to join him. She'd dressed in a pair of jeans, a dark green long-sleeved blouse, and carried a pair of black boots under one arm. "I take it all was quiet?"

"Yep. Not a thing out of place. Were you able to sleep?"

"I was. Thank you for staying, I doubt I could have otherwise." She sounded nonchalant, but he noted the pink that tinged her cheeks. After sitting down, she pulled the boots on and tied them.

They looked more like combat boots than anything else. Something about that made him smile. She'd never been one to wear the fancy shoes or anything with heels. He liked it.

Especially when she wasn't that much shorter than he was to begin with.

"There is one small problem," he announced. When she looked up in concern, he lifted the jar of instant coffee. "If this is what passes for coffee around here, we're going to need to make a pit stop on the way."

Paige grinned. "You won't hear an argument from me." She tugged at the hem of her blouse. "Let's go."

By the time they arrived at the Corner Café, Gabe's stomach was growling, and he figured Paige was probably hungry, too. He didn't have to do much convincing for her to let him buy her a cinnamon roll.

In the drive-thru, he accepted the two traveling cups of coffee and handed one to Paige.

She took a sip. Her eyes closed in pure bliss as every

muscle in her face seemed to relax at once. "So much better."

Gabe chuckled. "Anything is better than what you have at your house. You should invest in a coffee maker."

"Nah." She held the cup close to her face. "Well, maybe." She took another sip, then set her coffee in a cup holder. "If they'd been able to find Jane Dog's owner, would they have called you? Or me?"

"Not necessarily, especially since the investigation is ongoing." Gabe took a swig of his own coffee and nodded his approval. Dean Shaw, the owner of the café, was known in Destiny for some of the best coffee in town. That, and his cheeseburgers.

He accepted a bag from the lady at the drive-through window, then parked in a spot. He pulled a box from the bag, opened it, and handed it to Paige along with a fork. Warm frosting flowed over the sides of the cinnamon roll to pool in the bottom.

"Wow," Paige said as she admired her pastry. "These are huge." She used her fork to pull some of it away and took a bite. "How did I not know about these before?"

"They're good, right? Someone brought a box of them into the station last year. It got us all hooked." He took a generous bite of his own cinnamon roll. He pulled a small piece off and handed it to Loki, who gulped it and licked his lips in appreciation.

Gabe glanced at Paige. It was nice to spend some one-on-one time with her. Once Megan moved back to town, the four friends had started getting together again frequently. It was nearly the only time Gabe saw Paige.

"We should make a point to stay in touch with each other after Bryce and Megan are married."

Paige blinked at him in surprise. A moment later, a

shadow of sadness passed over her face just long enough for Gabe to notice before it disappeared. "I was thinking the other day about how things are probably going to change. Not intentionally, or even in a bad way. But it's going to be different."

He dragged a forkful of cinnamon roll through frosting before eating it. He hated the thought of going back to seeing Paige infrequently again. "Maybe you and I could have a standing breakfast meeting. You know, get coffee and cinnamon rolls every so often to stay in touch. Gossip about the new married couple." Gabe flashed his playful grin, but he hoped she'd seriously consider the possibility.

Paige stared at him as though she were trying to detect an underlying meaning to his suggestion. Finally, she nodded slowly. "I think that's a good idea. What about Mondays at six thirty? I'm almost never on call Sunday nights."

He hadn't expected her to agree so readily, or to something so regularly, either. "That should work for me, too." He had a suspicion Mondays would quickly become his favorite day of the week.

"Sounds good." Paige wiped her mouth with a napkin. "Are you sure it'll be okay for me to come into the station with you?"

Gabe nodded. "Absolutely. The chief and I are friends. Do you know Arnold Dolman? Anyway, he'll be at Bryce and Megan's wedding, too."

"Oh, that's right. I remember Bryce mentioning him." That seemed to satisfy her.

A short time later, they left the café parking lot with full bellies.

Gabe drove them across town to the police station

where a small crowd of people were standing on the sidewalk by the road, picket signs in hand.

Paige leaned forward in her seat. "What is that about?"

"They've been out here all week. Did you hear about the young man who was shot and killed a few weeks ago?"

"The news said it was tied to drug and gang activity."

"That's the one. Well, an undercover operation that had been ongoing for nearly a year managed to gather enough evidence to arrest Warren Teague as the leader of our local drug ring for a laundry list of drug charges." They'd known he was responsible for most of the meth coming in and out of Destiny for a while, but proving it hadn't been easy. Gabe drove through the parking lot and around behind the station to park.

"I remember reading about that."

"It's going to take a lot to make the charges stick. There are witnesses willing to come forward, but unfortunately one of them is the man who shot that teen. He's going to go to jail for what he did, but for now, we have to make sure he stays alive and hidden until we get Teague put away."

"Let me guess. A lot of people aren't happy about it."

"They want justice. And I get it, they deserve it. It'll come, but not as quickly as they'd like. So they take turns picketing to make sure we don't forget." He had to give them credit for their determination. If roles were reversed, he might do the same.

Once at the police station, he led Paige and Loki inside and to the chief's office. Chief of Police Arnold Dolman was bent over some paperwork on his desk when he looked up and saw them. He motioned them inside.

"Aren't you off shift, Gabe?"

"Yes, sir. This is Dr. Paige Wade, she's the veterinarian who was on staff last night at Destiny Animal Hospital."

"Of course. I don't think we've officially met, although we have several mutual friends." Arnold stood and reached to shake her hand. "Please, take a seat." He didn't regain his own until they'd both done as he asked. He kept his focus on Paige. "I was relieved to hear you weren't seriously injured in the attack."

"Thank you. It was a shock, that's for sure. I'm thankful officers showed up so quickly after my tech called it in."

"I'll have extra patrols go by the next few nights. Try to deter anyone from returning." Arnold shuffled some papers together and stacked them to his right.

"I appreciate that." Paige smiled then looked to Gabe for guidance on what to say next.

"Do we have any leads since this morning?" He reached down and patted Loki's head as the dog laid on the floor by his chair. "Any more information on the vehicle that the suspect may have used to escape?"

Arnold frowned. "None. It's like the guy is a ghost." He gave Paige an apologetic look.

Paige seemed disappointed but covered it quickly. "I appreciate all that your department is doing. I wish I had seen more to help identify the guy. He didn't speak a single word."

"Which makes me think this isn't his first rodeo," Gabe commented.

Arnold agreed. "And probably not his last. He was after something, and thanks to your quick thinking, Paige, he didn't succeed. There's a good chance he'll try something again. With any luck, we'll apprehend him soon."

Gabe glanced at Paige. "There is one more thing. Paige is certain someone followed her from the animal hospital to her own home when she got off work." He gave the chief a description of the car. "Later a similar car was parked in

43

front of her house. As soon as the driver saw she'd noticed him, it left."

"I never got a good look at the driver," Paige explained. "And the car didn't have a real license plate. Only those placeholders advertising the dealership they came from. This one said Bristow Ford and Dodge."

Arnold jotted some notes down and nodded approvingly. "I'll have someone go by the dealership and see if they've had any purchases matching this description. Maybe it'll give us a place to start." He took a swallow from the mug on his desk. "In the meantime, we're still looking for the vehicle and driver who dropped the dog off at your clinic. There were no reports of anyone matching his description showing up at a hospital needing medical help. But we've got everyone keeping an eye out. Something is going to turn up."

Gabe wasn't thrilled with the idea of dropping Paige off at her house and driving away. She insisted she was fine, and without further evidence that someone might be after her, he had no choice. He did make her promise to call him if the strange car showed up again.

He and Loki barely arrived at the precinct that evening to check in when Detective Paris found him in the hallway. "I thought you'd like to know that I followed up with the dealership. No cars reported stolen. They also haven't sold any vehicle matching that description in the last few months—certainly not recently enough to have their dealership tags still in place."

"So where did this car come from?" Had Paige misread the dealership tags?

Paris held up a hand. "Here's where things get a little interesting. A stack of those plates went missing a month or so ago. Gary Strider, the owner, said they eventually chalked it up to the plates being misplaced or possibly even thrown away."

"But now we're thinking someone swiped them."

"Yep. It's ingenious, really. Steal a car, take the old plates off, slap a dealership plate on. It's a lot less suspicious than running around without any plates at all, and no fake plates to run and identify. As long as they use them infrequently, that is."

This meant the car following Paige was most likely stolen. Her intuition had been spot-on. He knew she'd be glad to hear that.

It also meant that it'd be super easy to switch rides if whoever was responsible dealt in stolen vehicles. In fact, if the person who attacked and followed her had any measurable amount of intelligence, they'd have ditched the car by now simply because it'd been spotted.

Arnold came around the corner, a grim look on his face. He pointed at Gabe. "We've got an abandoned vehicle off the loop on the south side of town. It matches the description of the vehicle the dog's owner drove last night. No driver, but there is blood in the cab. The snowfall yesterday combined with all the runoff from most of it melting has made it difficult to find any trace of footprints or a blood trail." His phone trilled, and he glanced at it before continuing. "We may have an injured person in those woods. S&R has been working for a half hour or so, but I need you out there ASAP."

"Yes, sir." Gabe gave Paris a nod and jogged with Loki to make sure his vehicle was prepared.

Arnold had started the Destiny Search and Rescue

group several years ago. Most members were regular businessmen and women in town who were willing to volunteer to help their community. While Gabe wasn't technically a member himself, Loki had been helpful multiple times, especially when a missing person was involved.

By the time he arrived on the scene, a crowd of people had gathered as they created a search grid and assigned teams to each of the quadrants.

With this many people around, it would make it harder for Loki to sort through the scents. But if he could focus on the smell of blood, it would be easier to locate the injured driver.

"Come on, boy. Let's get to work."

The first thing they did was stop by the abandoned vehicle. Gabe studied it with a critical eye. There didn't seem to be any damage suggesting the driver had hit a tree or a deer. The driver side door was open wide.

Gabe took Loki up to the car and allowed him to smell the blood that covered part of the driver's seat. It wasn't a small amount, either. Maybe the driver was afraid he might lose consciousness, pulled over, and then became confused thanks to the newly fallen snow.

Gabe hoped they would be able to find the guy in time, although he had a sinking feeling that the odds weren't good.

"Alright, boy." He gave the dog the command to search.

Gabe allowed Loki a lot of leash so that he could freely inspect the blood and then begin to smell around the vehicle. It wasn't long before he took off in the direction of the woods, the only sound he made was the odd combination of squishing mud and slush beneath his paws and the huffs of air as he breathed.

Gabe spotted Officer Paul Krautscheid across the way

and motioned to Loki. Krautscheid nodded his understanding. No doubt he or another officer would be heading their way.

Loki raced through the snow, slowing only slightly as he caught another whiff, his ears erect and eyes keen on the ground in front of him. After a few minutes, he slowed, his attention wavering.

With no visual cues to look for, it was sometimes easy for Loki to miss where someone might have taken a turn because he was so focused on running forward.

Gabe brought him back to where he'd first started noticing Loki's change in demeanor and let him inspect the area for several minutes. To Gabe's relief, Loki took a sharp turn toward a small ridge at the top of a hill, his focus renewed.

As they neared the ridge, Loki paused a moment then barked. Gabe could see a body lying on the ground beneath a tree. He turned and cupped his hands around his mouth. "Over here!"

Gabe reined Loki in, then immediately rewarded him with his rope toy. "Good boy." He had no intention of getting any closer because he didn't want Loki to contaminate the scene.

Krautscheid approached from behind them, knelt beside the body, and felt for a pulse. He shook his head with a frown before speaking into his radio. "Driver of the abandoned vehicle has been found. DOA. Lots of visible blood. We need an ME down here." He gave specific directions to their location before turning to Gabe. "Good work. It could have been a while before S&R would've made it up here."

Too bad they couldn't have recovered the individual before it was too late. Although judging by the amount of blood in the car coupled with the exposed area of his arms and hands, Gabe suspected that the man might not have made it long anyway.

Less than ten minutes later, Arnold and the county's chief medical examiner, Genevieve Marks, approached the scene. The difference in height between the two would've been comical in a different situation.

Arnold, who stood at over six feet tall, practically dwarfed the red-headed Eve, who couldn't be more than five feet.

Arnold hung back with Gabe to give Eve room to work. Gabe didn't know her well, but he'd heard that, when busy with a body, she insisted on being able to focus completely. Other rumors suggested she was a force to be reckoned with if anyone messed with her crime scene.

"I've got people going through the car now," the chief said. "I'm guessing blood loss led to confusion, and that's why he wandered away from the road."

"With the fresh snowfall, it wouldn't have been hard to get disoriented. Especially after dark," Gabe added.

Arnold nodded his agreement.

Eve looked up at them. "You gentlemen would be right. I'll need to get the body back to the lab for a proper autopsy, but it looks like two stab wounds to the torso." She motioned for Krautscheid, who was standing nearby, to help her. They carefully turned the body so she could examine the back. "He bled out long before he would've died of exposure. He was likely suffering from extreme blood loss by the time he pulled his car off the road." They gently laid the body back down. She stood then, removed her gloves, and planted one hand on her hip. "I'll get you a more exact time of death, but based on liver temp, the snow covering the area, and what Chief Dolman told me of the incident at the vet clinic, I'd estimate it to be somewhere between ten and midnight last night."

She gave Krautscheid a nod. He knelt and went through the man's pockets and jacket. "I'm not finding a phone or a wallet. Maybe he was stabbed during a robbery or attempted carjacking?"

Arnold hooked a thumb through one of his belt loops. "Let's hope we get some information from the car that'll give us a clue about what happened to our John Doe here."

Eve stayed with the body, but Gabe pocketed Loki's rope toy and they walked with Arnold back down the hill. The sun was beginning to set, and with the clouds in the sky, it was getting dark fast. The predicted lows for the night would mean everything that melted would freeze over again.

"Hey, Chief." Another officer waved them over from the abandoned car. He opened a back door and motioned inside. "The whole seat is covered in dog hair. There's a coat with blood on it, too. I think it's safe to say this is the car from the clinic last night."

Gabe wasn't surprised. It sounded like the guy drove here right after dropping his dog off at the vet and then died from blood loss. But why this direction? Maybe blood loss had him disoriented. "I'll stop by and get a sample of fur from the dog to compare, just to be sure."

He went back to his Tahoe, secured Loki in the kennel in the back seat, and then dialed Paige's number.

She answered on the second ring. "Hey. Everything going okay?"

"I'm fine, but I've got some bad news. We located who we think is your patient's owner. He's dead—probably not too long after leaving the clinic last night."

All he heard was silence from her end of the line.

"Paige? You still there?"

"Yeah. Sorry, I'm still here. That's terrible." Her voice sounded sad.

"I need to get a sample of the dog's fur so we can make an official comparison. Is she still at the clinic?"

"Yes. I'm here visiting her, too. I was going to head home in a few minutes."

"Do me a favor? Stay there. I'll be by in a half hour or less." He started back toward the abandoned car.

"Sure, that's not a problem."

"Thanks, Paige." He hung up then and told the chief about the dog.

Arnold looked thoughtful. "Is the dog a purebred? Could she have been the reason why our John Doe was attacked in the first place? To steal her?"

"I'll ask Paige about that while I'm there."

"Let me know what you find out."

Gabe felt it was safe to assume that whoever killed the man they found today had also stabbed his dog. The motive for it was still a complete mystery, though. And until they uncovered that, it was impossible to know why someone was bothering Paige. But if it was the same person responsible for killing their John Doe, then as far as Gabe was concerned, Paige's life could be in danger, too.

Chapter Five

"That breaks my heart," Paige said as she ran a hand down Jane Dog's back. She'd gotten to think of her as JD now. Reg said that she'd done well enough through the night to remove her IV, but that she'd remained sad and lethargic. He finally called her to come in and see if being there made any difference.

The moment Paige stepped into the room, JD's tail thumped against the side of her kennel. She'd raised her chin and crinkled her eyes as though smiling. It was possible being there and helping her when she was so scared had created a bond that Paige hadn't anticipated.

Gabe arrived a few minutes earlier and collected some fur samples from JD to take back to the station. He pulled his phone out and paused. "I was wondering if you could look at a picture of the guy we found today. Let me know for sure that he's the one who dropped off the dog."

There was no missing the unspoken warning in his words. The picture he had to show her was of a dead man.

Paige swallowed but nodded. She needed to know for sure, too.

Gabe found the picture and handed her the phone.

One glance, and she immediately knew it was him. She gave a single nod and handed the phone back to him. "That's definitely the guy."

Who was dead. And probably not too long after he'd left the clinic.

Once again, Paige wished she'd looked past the injured dog and realized the man needed just as much help.

Her thoughts must have been showing on her face because Gabe touched her arm. "You have nothing to feel bad about. You couldn't have known. And even if you did call an ambulance, I don't think the guy would've waited around for it. He was running from something, Paige. You took care of the dog and saved her life. You did what you were supposed to do."

"So what happens next?" She opened the kennel door and cradled JD's head in her hands.

"We should have an identification on her owner soon. Once we do, we'll see if there's any next of kin. There may be someone to claim the dog."

If someone was out there who knew JD and would give her a good home, of course they needed to find them. But until then, Paige intended to watch over her.

JD wagged her tail, never taking her eyes off Paige's face.

"I think you're her hero, Paige."

No matter where Paige moved, JD's gaze stayed on her. "She was looking at me like that when she was first brought in. Those big, brown eyes are part of why I worked so hard to save her." She trailed a finger up the dog's muzzle and between her eyes before placing a kiss there. "You know, I always care about my patients. I try not to get overly attached to some of them. But this girl here..." Memories of

Pepper converged with what JD must have gone through before she was brought in, and the result was a sudden urge to cry.

She swallowed a lump in her throat and blinked back tears.

Gabe placed a warm hand on her shoulder. "If no one steps forward to claim her, maybe you should keep her yourself."

She hadn't been able to fathom getting another dog after Pepper. But there was something about JD... "Yeah, I think I might." She cleared her throat. "You'll keep me updated?"

"Of course." There was something in the tone of his voice that snagged her attention.

Gently, Paige nudged JD back into her crate and closed the door before turning to face him. "What is it?"

"The man we found was stabbed twice. Likely by the same person who cut JD." He held a hand out, and JD gave it a quick nuzzle. "Can you tell if the dog is a pure bred? Is it possible that someone may have seen her and killed the owner in hopes of stealing her? Maybe to sell her later?"

Paige immediately shook her head. "I seriously doubt that. She does seem to be pure bred. But she's spayed, which means she can't be a breeder even if she did come from champion lines. She's also incredibly docile with no evidence to suggest she was ever used in dog fights. I can't imagine why someone would want to steal her."

Gabe nodded thoughtfully. "That's a good thing. She was probably in the wrong place at the wrong time, then."

"Then what's the connection between what happened to them, and the guy who tried to get my keys last night? Or who followed me home?"

"I wish I knew. Chances are, someone stabbed our John Doe, who then managed to get away with whatever his attacker wanted. Maybe they thought you knew where he went, or that John Doe gave you something when he dropped off the dog." Gabe shrugged. "I'm hoping that, once we get an ID on the guy and make an official state-ment, his attacker will realize he's dead now and back off."

"What are the odds of that?" The question came out before Paige had the chance to think it through. Just because she was nervous someone might approach her again didn't mean Gabe should feel responsible for holding her hand until the case was solved.

"We're working on all the angles. Meanwhile, we've got patrols going by here regularly, and we've increased police presence on your street as well." He reached out and gave her arm a gentle squeeze. "I need to get this sample back to the station, and it's getting dark outside. Are you heading home?"

"Yes, and I'm bringing JD back with me. She needs to be watched closely, and at least then Reg won't have to stay here tonight unless another emergency comes up."

"Why don't I help you get everything loaded into your car? Then I can follow you home and make sure you get there okay."

"That would be great, thank you." Between Paige, Gabe, and one of the techs, they got JD carefully trans-ferred along with medical supplies and food.

At her place, Gabe again helped her get everything inside. JD looked about her new surroundings curiously, but it didn't take long for her to settle on the thick cushion on the floor and close her eyes.

"I appreciate the help." Paige walked Gabe to the front door. "Will you let me know what you find out about JD?"

"I'll keep you updated. And you have to promise me

that you'll call if you need anything, no matter what. Okay?"

"Sure."

"Paige." His voice, which was normally laid back or playful, took on a more serious note. "I mean it."

"I called you this morning, didn't I? If something else happens, I've got your number on speed dial."

That seemed to satisfy him.

She locked the door behind him, then went to check on JD again. The dog had a long recovery ahead of her, but even knowing that, Paige felt safer with her there.

Since the poor dog's owner was deceased, part of Paige hoped that things would work out so she could keep JD. Maybe that meant she was finally ready to open her heart and home to a new dog.

Gabe frowned at the man's face on the computer screen. "Samuel Finch," he said aloud. While there had been no wallet on the man they'd found dead in the woods, they were able to locate registration papers in the car's glove compartment. That led to the identification of their victim.

Although it was clear that he was no saint.

Paris nodded then clicked a button to switch the screen from the picture to a long list of charges. "He's served time for robbery, possession of a controlled substance with intent to sell, and multiple DUIs. It looks like he's either been clean or lying low since he got out on probation three years ago."

Gabe felt rather than saw Loki sit at his side. He put a hand on the dog's head. "Possession of a controlled substance. Any direct connection with the local drug cartel?"

"None. When he went on parole, he never missed an appointment with his parole officer." Paris shrugged. "Even before that, he was a relatively small fish."

"Judging from the stab wounds, either looks are deceiving, or his past caught up with him." Gabe scratched the back of his neck. "Have we heard back from the lab about the dog hair?"

Paris nodded. "It is a match. However, Finch doesn't have any next of kin outside of a cousin that we could find, and the cousin didn't want anything to do with Finch or his dog. Said he hadn't talked to him in over ten years."

That meant, if Paige chose to, she could keep JD. He thought that would make her happy. "Alright, let's head downstairs and see if Eve has been able to learn anything else from our victim."

The moment they reached the doorway to the morgue, Eve looked up and gave them a smile. "Welcome, gentlemen. Right on time. I was finishing up with Mr. Finch here." She waved a hand toward the body on her table that was covered with a plastic sheet.

Eve always treated the bodies in her morgue with the utmost respect, which was something Gabe appreciated. In fact, it wasn't unusual for someone to walk into the morgue to find Eve conversing with one of her patients as though they were alive and well.

Gabe motioned for Loki to lie down in the doorway of the room. The dog obeyed immediately, but never turned his attention from Gabe.

Eve tightened her ponytail before reaching for the chart nearby. "Mr. Finch died due to blood loss after receiving two stab wounds here," she pointed, "and here. He's lucky he made it as far as he did before the blood loss caused him to lose consciousness." She showed the information about the type of knife that might have been used. "By the time he pulled the car over to the side of the road, the loss of blood would have resulted in confusion. No doubt that's why we found his body up by the ridge."

"Were you able to run a toxicology panel?" Paris asked.

"I did, and it came back clean. No evidence of recent drug use." She flipped to a different page on the chart. "He did have stage two Hepatocellular carcinoma. Liver cancer. I don't see any evidence to suggest that he was being treated for it. It could be he didn't even know yet. But you might dig into his records. Maybe he was seeing a doctor."

Gabe made notes to do exactly that. "Thanks, Eve."

She grinned then and held up a finger to stop them. "I have one more piece of interesting news." She reached for a small tray that held some coins, a pack of gum, and a pocketknife. "These are all of Mr. Finch's possessions. As you know, his wallet was missing. However, these were found in his pockets." With a finger, she moved objects around until she singled out a half dollar. "I originally tossed this coin in with the rest of his things. But then I noticed something odd."

Gabe and Paris followed her to the other side of the room where she brought a mounted magnifying glass down, flipped on a light, and centered it over the coin.

"I noticed this lip around the coin. You see it here?" She pointed to the slight raised area on the edge of the coin. It reminded Gabe of the gold chocolate coins that he used to get in his stocking at Christmas every year. "So I pulled it apart and check this out." She demonstrated by snapping the top of the coin away from the bottom. "Voila!" Inside, nestled in the bottom of the coin, was an SD card.

"I had no idea there was such a thing." Gabe reached for the coin and admired it before handing it to Paris. "Awesome find."

"Thank you. And for the curious, you can buy half dollars with hidden compartments online for cheaper than you'd think." She placed a hand on one hip. "I may have to get one for myself just because it's cool."

Gabe might do the same. "We'll get this to tech so they can see if there's anything on it that might help with the motive to kill Finch."

"Sounds good. Let me know, will you? I'm picturing all kinds of spy scenarios."

Gabe chuckled. "Will do."

Eve reached for a jar on the counter and opened it, retrieving a dog biscuit. "May I?" she asked, pointing to Loki who was still waiting in the doorway.

Gabe nodded his approval. Loki happily accepted the biscuit from Eve and ate it, giving his lips an approving lick when it was gone. She ran a hand over Loki's head and earned herself a kiss from the dog.

"Thanks, Eve," Paris said as they made their way out. "Great work as always."

"Just doing my job."

Paris held up the SD card. "Let's go see what tech can find."

As they left the room, Gabe could hear Eve speaking to the corpse again.

"All right, Mr. Finch, let's get you transferred to refrigeration..."

Chapter Six

"I have no idea what's on it," Logan Alcott announced with a frown. He glared at the SD card held between his thumb and first finger. "The data is encrypted."

Gabe had hoped Logan, one of their best tech wizards, would be able to pull information off the SD card. He'd considered the possibility that anything on it might be entirely unhelpful to their case. But he hadn't anticipated being unable to see the contents at all.

"There's no way you can crack the code, or whatever it is that computer experts do?" Paris took the card and looked at both sides.

"It requires a passcode, which I don't have." Logan held up both hands. "But if you can do whatever it is that detectives do and get me that passcode, then we'll be in business."

Paris chuckled. "Fair enough." He turned to Gabe. "We should have no trouble obtaining a warrant for Finch's place, but it'll most likely come through tomorrow. With any luck, we'll find the code there. You up for joining me, Harrison?"

Gabe loved his job and the freedom he and Loki had when it came to helping his fellow officers. But there were times when detective work held some appeal. Opportunities like this were the chance to do both. "Sounds like a plan." He hoped the SD card was the reason why Finch was stabbed. The idea that it may have nothing at all to do with Paige made him feel a lot better.

He shook hands with Paris, thanked Logan, and headed out of the IT department. "Come on, boy, it's time we get back out there."

Once Gabe had Loki settled in the Tahoe and got in himself, he dialed Paige's number.

She answered quickly. "Hey, Gabe."

"Hey, yourself. How are you doing?"

"I'm good. I'm at home, and Megan came over to watch a movie." She laughed at something in the background.

That's right, they were having their girls' night. He'd make the phone call short. Gabe smiled at the thought of the two ladies relaxing and having fun together. It was something Paige needed after everything she'd gone through.

"Well, I have good news for you. JD is all yours if you want her."

"Are you serious?" Paige sounded surprised.

"Her owner had no next of kin. There's no one to take the dog in." He thought she might be more obviously excited. Instead, there was nothing but silence. "Paige? You still there?"

A sniff came over the phone. "Yeah, I'm here. Sorry, I'm just sad for her. But I'm happy that JD can stay here. Hey, do you happen to know what her name is?"

"I don't, but we're going over to look at the owner's house tomorrow. I'll see if anything has her name on it, and make sure to pick up any of her toys. Maybe that'll help her adjust."

"That'll be great." Paige sounded relieved. "Thank you for thinking of it."

"You're welcome." He paused, imagining her at the house with their friend. He was glad she wasn't alone. "Is Megan staying all night?"

"No, she'll probably head home after we finish our movie."

There was something in her voice that caught Gabe's attention. Was she worried about being home alone tonight? "I'll be on patrol until late. If you need something, call me."

"Thanks, Gabe."

"You're welcome. Now go watch your chick flick and have fun."

"I will." There was a moment of silence. "Be careful, Gabe."

"Yes, ma'am." He imagined her rolling her eyes at him which only made him smile. "Bye, Paige."

"Bye."

"You like him." There was no teasing tone to Megan's voice. Her statement was simply that—a fact.

Paige had hung up with Gabe to find Megan watching her thoughtfully. "We're friends. Have been for almost as long as you and me. I sure hope I like him."

"Funny." Megan sat on the floor, her back against the couch.

Paige had to get her cell phone from the kitchen counter where she'd left it. She brought it back and regained her spot on the floor near her friend. JD slept soundly between them. She needed to give the dog a more personalized name.

It was nearly impossible to hide anything from Megan. Especially now that she lived in Destiny again and they didn't have to rely on virtual conversation to stay in touch. Megan had been aware of how much Paige cared about Gabe back in school. She'd also known how devastating it was for Paige to lose her brother and uncle in the line of duty in the course of two weeks, and the effect it had on Paige. "It doesn't matter how much I like him. We're just friends."

"I have a pretty good feeling he'd jump at the chance to change that if he had even the slightest hint that you'd be open to it." Megan chose a licorice whip from the candy charcuterie board she'd brought along and handed it to Paige.

Paige took a large bite and then pressed play on the remote control to continue their movie. She'd lost count of how many times they'd watched *While You Were Sleeping* together. But it was funny, sweet, and romantic. Not to mention seeing it frequently meant they could enjoy it while still visiting as much as they wanted to. The perfect combination.

"You know how I feel about the idea of marrying someone with that kind of job. Wondering every day if something was going to happen ... I couldn't do it." She realized how that sounded when her friend was about to marry a firefighter. "I'm sorry. I'm not trying to be all doom and gloom. This is supposed to be your night to relax and giggle about your husband-to-be. I just need to shut up."

Megan grabbed a handful of peanut M&Ms and ate them one by one as she watched the movie. Finally, she turned to face Paige. "You don't think I worry about that with Bryce? Every time I see a fire truck go by, I wonder if he's on it. When I hear about a burning building, I worry he's going to have to run into it to save someone else. But being a firefighter is who he is. Is it dangerous? You bet it can be. It's also part of what makes him so caring. I love that he's willing to do what it takes to save the lives of others. And if, God forbid, something ever does happen, he'll go down doing what he feels he's called to do." Her voice broke.

Paige reached across the dog and clasped her best friend's hand. "You are one of the strongest people I've ever known." Megan had survived a childhood riddled with abuse at the hand of her father. Instead of letting that dictate the course of her life, she'd become a successful pediatric nurse. "Seriously, you and Bryce are perfect for each other. There aren't many people who see you guys and don't think to themselves, 'Relationship goals, right there.'"

JD shifted, her fur tickling the bottom of Paige's wrist. She let go of her friend's hand and chose another piece of candy.

There were several minutes where only sounds of the movie filled the room. Megan spoke up again. "How much longer does Gabe have before the end of his shift?"

Paige looked at her watch. "About five and a half hours." The moment the words came out of her mouth, and she saw the smug look on her friend's face, she knew she'd walked into a trap. "Watch the movie—we're almost to your favorite part."

Megan ignored the TV screen completely. "So let me get this straight. You know exactly when his shifts begin and when they end." When Paige didn't correct her, Megan continued. "Do you worry about him? Wonder how his day is going?"

Annoyance sparked. "What's your point, Megan?"

"My point is, it seems to me you're doing all the worrying and wondering anyway, without any of the benefits. Despite everything you've tried to do to avoid it." She smiled then, a kind smile without a single hint of pity or humor. "He's the real deal. Bryce told me he spent last night here on the couch so you could get some sleep. Believe me when I say that is some kind of sacrifice." She poked the couch as though she half expected it to come alive. "And don't tell me it was just part of his job, because we both know that's not true."

Megan reached over and fake punched her friend's arm. "I wish you could let yourself see that all the good that could exist between you and Gabe would completely overshadow the worry. It won't disappear, but it'll be manageable. Because you'll be there for each other."

"And if things don't work out? Aside from you, Gabe is my closest friend. The thought of something ruining that..." Paige groaned, the sound drawing JD's attention. The sweet girl looked up with concern before settling again, her head resting across Paige's lap. She needed a change of subject. "Now that I'm going to keep this crazy dog, she needs a better name. At least until we can figure out what her real name is."

Megan motioned to the movie. "What about Lucy?" she asked, referring to the main character in *While You Were Sleeping*.

"That's not a bad idea." She rubbed one of the dog's ears between her finger and thumb. "Lucy! What do you think of that name? Lucy!"

The dog lifted her head and tilted it slightly.

Megan laughed. "I'd say that's a yes."

"Then Lucy it is." Paige grinned. Keeping the dog seemed so much more official now.

"Maybe we're asking ourselves the wrong question here."

"Oh? What do you mean?"

Megan's eyes glittered with amusement. "Before you even think about Gabe being more than a friend, maybe you should see how well Lucy and Loki get along." Her eyes widened. "Oh, my goodness, the names even sound good together. Now that is cute."

Paige wanted to be annoyed, but she couldn't force it. Instead, she chuckled at her friend's antics. "A valid question." Somehow, she had a feeling the dogs would get along just fine. She put her phone on the coffee table and moved Lucy's head to the floor. "I should get her antibiotics before it gets much later. You can leave the movie playing, I'll be right back."

Lucy opened her eyes enough to see Paige walk away before closing them again. Hopefully, she would start gaining more strength over the next few days. Again, Paige was glad that she could keep the dog with her instead of worrying about her at the clinic overnight.

After giving Lucy her medication, she enjoyed settling in with Megan for the rest of the movie, laughing when poor on-screen Lucy had to prove her engagement to Peter, and then sighing at the end when Jack proposed to her in front of his family. "I will never get tired of watching that movie," Paige said as she stood up to eject the DVD.

"Me, either. They don't make movies like that anymore." Megan groaned as she stood from the floor. "Oh, my goodness, I ate way too much candy. I can hear my aunt warning me that I won't fit into my wedding dress if I keep this up." She laughed hard at that.

"Unless the dress barely fit you to start with, I think it'd take more than one night of candy to make a difference."

"I have no doubt that you're right." She glanced at her watch. "I suppose I should be getting home. Mom keeps telling me to make sure I get enough sleep so I don't have bags under my eyes for wedding pictures."

"I'll take this in the kitchen and put all of the candy in baggies."

Paige had barely picked up the tray of treats when Lucy's head shot up and a growl erupted low in her throat. The sound made Paige fumble. The platter hit the coffee table and several pieces of candy bounced out and onto the wooden surface.

Lucy growled again and got to her feet. The injury didn't seem to slow her down at all. She crossed the room and stood before the front door. The hair along the back of her neck bristled.

"I'm betting she hasn't done that before," Megan said, her attention moving from the dog to her friend, her eyes wide.

"No, she hasn't." It wasn't until she spoke that Paige realized she'd been holding her breath. "I'm going to call Gabe."

Megan only nodded her agreement.

Thankfully, Gabe answered on the first ring. "I didn't figure I'd hear from you until tomorrow—"

"I think someone's sneaking around outside the house."

Chapter Seven

Gabe immediately took a turn and sped up. "I'm two blocks away. I'll be right there. What makes you think someone's outside?"

"Lucy—JD—is standing in front of the door growling and clearly in defensive mode, despite her injuries." Paige paused. "I could try and look out of the kitchen window to see if anyone is out there."

"No. Stay away from the door and windows. I'm less than three minutes away." He announced where he was going on the radio. "Don't hang up until I get there."

The dog barked in the background, and he heard Paige's breath catch.

"I hate not feeling secure in my own house," she said, her voice shaky.

"I know. I'm on your street. I'm not coming in with lights so I can see if anyone is there."

Paige didn't respond. Gabe parked and then went around and let Loki out of his kennel. Together, they quietly approached Paige's house.

There was no movement at all, and the lack of a breeze

intensified the quiet. Further down the street, a car pulled away from the curb and drove off in a hurry. "I don't see anyone, but a car several houses down just raced away. Don't unlock the door yet, I'm going to check around your place first."

"Please be careful." Paige's voice sounded strained.

Gabe took his flashlight out and turned it on, immediately spotting a set of footprints in the mud near the front door. They continued across the front of the house, around the side, then to the back. After that, whoever was there seemed to double back and from the side of the house walk toward the neighbor's yard in the same direction as the car that he saw leave earlier.

There was no doubt in his mind that someone had been casing Paige's house. Anger sparked at the thought of anyone trying to spy on her or make her uncomfortable. If the dog hadn't barked and scared the man away, would he have tried to break in?

Gabe would love to catch the guy in the act.

He spoke into the phone, "Everything's clear. I'm coming to the front door."

Paige was ready to open it the moment he knocked and ushered him and Loki inside. He didn't miss the way she immediately locked the door again behind him. They both hung up their phones.

Megan tipped her head toward Lucy. "You should've seen her, Gabe. I'm pretty sure she'd have torn someone apart if they'd come in. But then, suddenly, she returned to normal when she heard you guys outside, and she started wagging her tail."

The three of them watched as the two dogs immediately began sniffing each other.

"I wish I'd taken a video of Lucy and the way she was

growling," Paige said. "She's still in a lot of pain, but she didn't hesitate to guard the door."

Gabe made sure to lavish Lucy with praise. Knowing she was such a good watch dog made him feel better about Paige being home alone tonight. "I didn't see anyone out there. But there are fresh footprints in the mud going up to your front door and all the way around to the back of the house."

Paige pulled her arms tight against her chest. "The idea that they might have been trying to look inside..." She shivered, then reached for a light jacket that was draped over a nearby chair. She pulled it on. "I may never open my curtains or blinds again."

She should be able to feel safe in her own home. The fact that someone had taken that away from her made Gabe more than a little angry.

"Do you think your landlord would go for having a security system installed?" The question came from Megan.

"I'm not sure. I guess I could ask. I know the landlord won't foot the bill for it, and I'm not sure I can afford it right now. I may call him anyway."

Gabe nodded his approval. The simple presence of security cameras might create a deterrent on their own.

He looked over to see that Lucy had lain down again, probably exhausted after playing her part as a guard dog. Loki claimed a spot on the floor near her.

Megan nudged Paige in the side. "I guess there's an answer to one of your questions." There was no missing the amusement in her eyes.

"Hush," was all Paige said in return.

Megan full on giggled, leaving Gabe to wonder what he'd missed. Judging by the way Paige blushed as she avoided eye contact with him, he suspected it had something to do with him.

"I was about to head home," Megan told Gabe.

"Oh, yes. The sweets." Paige snatched up the largest candy platter Gabe had ever seen.

"Wow. I could learn a thing or two about movie night from you ladies. That's impressive."

Paige held it out so he could grab a piece. "It's all Megan. She's got skills." She bagged everything up and handed it to her best friend.

Gabe told Loki to stay. "I'll walk you out to your car, Megan. Make sure you get on your way okay."

"I appreciate it." She turned to give Paige a hug. "I had so much fun. We'll have to do this regularly, even after Bryce and I are married."

"Absolutely." The tightness in Paige's voice revealed her emotion. She cleared her throat. "I'll see you on Saturday morning to help you get ready."

"I'll be right back," Gabe said, then held the door open for Megan before closing it again behind them. Once she was safely in her car and pulling away, he returned to the house to find Paige snapping a picture of their dogs with her phone.

"They're being cute," she said in way of an explanation, as though she needed to justify taking a photo.

"Yes, they are." So was she, standing there in her baggy shirt and oversized lounge pants. Her hair was pulled into a messy bun that looked like it might tumble down at any moment.

"You need to get back to work, don't you?"

He did. He still had a good part of his shift ahead of him. But he also had several things he wanted to talk to Arnold about, and he intended to do that from his vehicle in front of her house where he could keep an eye on it. But she didn't need to know that, otherwise she'd insist she didn't need someone there watching her.

"Lock the door as soon as I leave. Don't open it for anyone unless you know for sure who it is. Keep the blinds and curtains closed—"

"Oh, trust me, I will."

"—and keep your cell phone handy. If Lucy gets worked up about anything, call me right away."

Paige's pretty, brown eyes widened, but she nodded her agreement. She reached a hand toward him but pulled it back again. "Be careful. Please."

"Says the woman with the stalker." He meant it as a tease and smiled, but she only frowned.

"I'm serious, Gabe."

He stepped forward and put his arms around her in a gentle hug. A few strands of hair fell from her bun and tickled his nose as the scent of her shampoo enveloped him. "I'm always careful."

She nodded, then slipped her arms around his waist to return the hug.

It was impossible not to acknowledge how perfectly she fit in his arms. If something happened to her ... he couldn't imagine his life without her in it.

He began to pray out loud. "Father God, we ask that you place a hedge of protection around Paige, her home, and around me as well. Give us wisdom, guide everyone who is working on this case, and help us to find the person responsible. Thank you for your love and protection. In the name of Jesus we pray, amen."

"Amen," Paige echoed, then leaned away from Gabe enough to look up at him. "Thank you."

"You're welcome." He let his arms drop as a call came over his radio. "I'd better get going. I'll call you later?"

"Please. At least when you get off shift."

"Don't forget to—"

"Lock the door behind you. I remember." She raised an eyebrow at him.

Gabe chuckled. "Right. Come on, Loki. Let's go, boy."

Loki groaned as he stretched before trotting to stand next to his owner. Reluctantly, Gabe left the house, waiting long enough to hear the lock slide into place behind him before stepping off the porch.

Gabe's hug threw Paige completely off balance. It was the last thing she ever would have expected him to do. Although maybe even more bewildering was the way being close to him had filled her with warmth and a sense of safety. She'd felt the loss when he stepped away as surely as the cooler air had surrounded her again.

She thought about what Megan said earlier about how Paige was invested in Gabe's safety. Her best friend wasn't wrong. Tonight, she wouldn't be able to rest easily until she knew he was off shift, and she wouldn't know that until he called her. Assuming he remembered.

If they were married, she'd know because he'd be walking into the house again, unscathed. The irony of that wasn't lost on Paige.

She allowed herself to flop onto the couch and then reach down to pet Lucy. "What do you think, girl? Any objections to staying with me?" The dog was nearly asleep again and barely opened one eye to look at her. "I'll take that as a no."

She turned on the TV and found some reruns of one of her favorite shows, which barely lasted an hour before Paige was back on her feet pacing again.

Lucy groaned as though she wished Paige would sit still for a while.

"Sorry, girl. I guess I'm a little restless."

She cleaned the kitchen, then found herself staring at the blinds covering one of the front windows. Nothing was out of place, and Lucy didn't seem worried about anything, but all Paige could imagine was someone standing on the other side of that window.

"God, I desperately need an extra helping of your peace right now." Paige breathed in and out several times to steady her heart rate. "I know I'm being paranoid. There's no way someone would be stupid enough to come back after hearing Lucy bark and then seeing Gabe come by."

As if to prove to herself that she was right, she sidled up beside the window and slowly pulled the blinds down at the edge to peer outside.

The first thing she saw was Gabe's Tahoe parked right in front of her house. Relief flooded her system, and a smile lifted the corners of her mouth. She let the blinds snap back into place.

Paige sat on the couch again, phone in hand, and texted Gabe.

"What are you doing outside my house? Don't you have somewhere else to be?"

"Nope."

"You can't stay out there all night."

"Want to bet?"

Paige's eyes narrowed. Was he serious?

> "I'm going to bring you some hot chocolate."

> "You don't need to do that, Paige. I'm just doing my job."

> "And so am I. If you get frostbite out there, you'll never let me forget it."

> "Then let me know when it's ready, and I'll come to the door. You don't need to get out in this cold weather."

She sent a thumbs-up emoji and started warming milk in the microwave. She might skimp on coffee, but she only bought one particular brand of hot chocolate mix that she found to be exceptionally rich and creamy. She spooned a generous amount of powder into each of the two travel mugs on the counter.

Once she'd added the milk and mixed them well, she put the lids on and texted Gabe.

Less than a minute later, she heard a light knock on the door followed by Gabe's voice. "It's me."

Paige unlatched the door and pulled it open. She handed him a mug and watched as he took a sip of the hot liquid and nodded his appreciation. "That's some of the best hot chocolate I've ever had."

"Thanks." She paused. "Are you serious about staying out there all night?"

"I am. I cleared it with the chief, and I'm going to be watching your house at night when I'm on duty until we catch this guy."

"And when you're not working?"

"Then I'm going to be keeping an eye on my friend to make sure no one messes with her."

Paige shook her head in disbelief. "I don't know what to say. Is there any way I can convince you that I'm okay, and that you can at least go home and get some sleep when your shift is over?"

"Not a thing." He took another sip of his hot chocolate, but his gaze never left hers. "I'll sleep tomorrow while you're at work."

"Fine. If you're going to be my self-appointed body-guard, then you and Loki might as well come inside." There was no way staying in his Tahoe for an extended time like that would be comfortable.

"You're not worried about sharing your house, even if it takes a day or two to solve this case and to catch your attacker?"

Why didn't he look as surprised by her offer as she felt? "If it means you're not sitting out there in your truck all night, then no, I'm not worried." Except that wasn't entirely true, was it? It was easy to keep her emotions in check when they saw each other casually from time to time. But having him stay in her house was a whole different scenario.

Gabe grinned at her over the rim of his cup.

"What? What's so funny?"

His amusement shifted to a sheepish look. "I was kind of banking on you extending the invitation. One of the other officers watched your house while I went to get some clothes, food for Loki, and some camping gear."

"Camping gear?" Now she was confused.

"There's absolutely no way I'm sleeping on that horrible couch of yours. A bedroll on the floor will be more comfort-able any day of the week."

Irritation flared as Paige glared at him. "Nice to know I'm so predictable."

"No, not predictable." He sobered. "Kind. Ready to help anyone else that needs it. Unwilling to see someone suffer, even if that includes your crazy friend sitting in his heated Tahoe." He gave her a wink and another smile.

Her exasperation subsided a little. The man knew just how powerful his wink was, especially when he paired it with that unbeatable smile. It was impossible to stay mad at him for long. She took a step back and tilted her head toward the living room. "Come on."

Chapter Eight

Paige shut her alarm off at six thirty the next morning. It took several moments for her brain to fully wake up, and then she bolted upright in her bed as memories of the evening before came flooding back.

When she went to bed last night, she'd fully expected to have a hard time sleeping. But knowing that Gabe was in the living room with Loki had apparently put her at ease because the moment her head hit the pillow, she must have fallen asleep.

She leaned over the edge of the bed to check on Lucy who was lying on a blanket on the floor.

The dog looked up at her, tail thumping the floor and eyes nearly crinkled with happiness.

"Hey, sweetie." Paige eased herself onto the floor beside her and put an arm around the dog's neck. "How are you feeling?" She ran a hand over the dog's side. It didn't seem warm, which hopefully meant they were continuing to avoid infection. Once they got to the animal hospital, she'd change the bandage and get a good look at the wound.

Lucy ate up the attention.

As she got ready for the day, Paige could hear noises coming from the living room and knew that Gabe was up and moving around. Had he slept at all?

She opened the door to find Loki sitting there waiting for them. The two dogs greeted each other, then left her behind as they trotted into the kitchen.

Gabe's sleeping bag was folded into a pile on the floor behind the couch. If her couch truly was that uncomfortable, maybe it was time to get a new one. She'd consider the possibility once this case was in her rearview mirror.

"Good morning," Gabe said after leaning partway into the living room from the kitchen. "Did you sleep okay?"

"Actually, yeah, I did. I don't think I even moved last night."

"That's good." He disappeared, and she followed him into the kitchen where he was unpacking food and setting it on the little table. "I took the liberty of having breakfast delivered today."

Paige noted the hashbrown bites along with ham, egg, and cheese sandwiches. He'd even thought to include coffee. "Wow, this looks amazing. Thank you."

"Not a problem." Once they were both sitting at the table, he said a prayer over their meal.

She took a sip of her coffee and sighed happily. "So good."

"I'm going to talk to Bryce and Megan about going in together to buy you a coffee machine. So act surprised at Christmas, okay?"

With a chuckle, she held the cup up. "Deal." They started on their sandwiches. "Did you get any sleep?"

"A few hours. Everything was quiet last night. I spoke with dispatch, and there were no reports of suspicious activity from the officers who patrolled your neighborhood.

I'd like to think having a police vehicle parked out front would deter most individuals."

"I should certainly hope so." She popped a hashbrown bite in her mouth and chewed thoughtfully.

"How are your parents doing?"

They'd moved to Arizona a year after Paige graduated from high school. Paige considered joining them after graduating college, but working with Reg at the animal hospital was too good of an opportunity to pass up. Besides, Destiny would always be home. At least they came back once a year to visit, and she made it to their place for Christmas. "They're doing well. Staying busy. Dad works for the city, and Mom is huge into volunteering. I think she volunteers more hours a week than most people work. But it keeps her busy, so that's good." It'd been Mom's way of coping after the death of her brother, Tommy.

"I'm glad to hear that. They were always good people. I missed seeing them around once they moved."

Paige nodded but didn't know what to say. The night when a knock on the door ushered in the news of her brother's death while stationed in Afghanistan forced its way into her mind. She needed to change the subject. "What are you going to be doing while I'm at work today?"

"As soon as you leave for the clinic, I'll head to the station. I want to check in with Detective Paris. Hopefully he'll get a search warrant for Finch's house first thing this morning. If we can find the passcode to the SD card Finch had, maybe we can piece together why he was killed. Then either make a connection between that and the guy who keeps bothering you or prove that they have nothing in common."

"Either way, I wish I knew what this guy wanted. The fact he tried to take my keys when he initially attacked me made me think he wanted access to something. My first thought was the medication in the clinic. But if he's tied to Finch and Lucy, there has to be more to it than that."

"Agreed. The behavior doesn't present itself like a typical stalker, either. We're missing a big piece of this puzzle."

They ate for several minutes in silence. Both dogs followed every single bite with their eyes, and Gabe and Paige finally relented, giving each of them a small piece of egg.

"You're a good girl, Lucy." She gave the dog a pat.

"Does the new name mean you're keeping her for sure?"

"It does."

Gabe gave her a warm smile. "I'm glad. She's one lucky pup." He finished his sandwich and leaned back in his chair. "Are you on call tonight?"

"No. I spoke with Reg, and he's calling in a favor with another veterinarian friend of his. I'm not on call at all until Saturday night. Reg is going out of town that day. I'll bring lunch to the clinic with me today, so I don't have to go anywhere at noon. If yesterday was any indication, Reg will walk with me out to the car this evening when I get off work."

"Good. I'll be waiting here for you when you get home. Do you have any takeout requests for dinner?"

She eyed him curiously. He'd always been sure of himself, but she hadn't really seen him take command of a situation like this. Maybe she should balk a little, but truthfully, it felt good to know he cared enough to be there for her. "I've been craving fried chicken."

"Good choice. Okay, I'll have that here waiting when you get home, too."

Paige chuckled. "I feel like this is the part in a football game where the team is strategizing right before they yell, 'Go team!'" As soon as she spoke the words, she knew exactly where Gabe was going to go with his teasing comeback.

"We'll be sure to stay away from the butt pats." His grin widened as he raised a single eyebrow.

"Far, far away," she replied as she pointed a finger at him.

Gabe was thankful that, even though he wasn't on duty yet, Paris still invited him to tag along to check out Finch's place. It was a modest place but well maintained on the outside and practically spotless inside.

They spent several hours searching for the passcode or any other information that might bring them one step closer to figuring out why someone would want to kill Finch and where the SD card fit in with it all.

Gabe also kept an eye out for some indication of what Lucy's real name was. There were plenty of dog toys strewn around the house, but nothing with a name on it.

In the end, he bagged up the dog's food and water bowls, dog bed, and a variety of toys that he hoped would make her feel more at home.

Now he and Paris were back at the station to let everyone know what they did—or didn't—find.

"We couldn't locate a passcode anywhere in Finch's house." Paris sat across the conference table from the chief. Along with the two of them were Gabe, Krautscheid, and several other officers. "Of course, if it was written on a slip of paper somewhere, it might have been impossible to find.

We brought back a sizable stack of papers we'll go through here just in case."

"What about the computer?" Arnold asked. "Did you find anything else on it?"

"Now that's the interesting part." Paris leaned closer to the table. "There was no computer in Finch's house. There wasn't even a place that looked like it was set up for a computer."

Gabe thought most people had a computer of some kind in their homes. "And his cell phone is still off?"

"That's correct." Paris pulled out his notes. "According to phone records, the last outgoing call was the one to Paige Wade's house. Since then, it's been powered off which means we've had no luck pinging its location. At this point, it's likely been tossed. If the passcode was stored on it..."

Arnold looked thoughtful. "What was a man who is clearly not into tech doing with an SD card?"

"And why was it hidden inside a false coin?" The question came from Krautscheid.

"If I had to guess," began Paris, "he was the go-between. Let's assume there's something valuable on the card. Maybe he received it from someone, was supposed to meet a buyer, and then was killed before the exchange took place."

"That seems like a stretch," Krautscheid objected. "How do we know he didn't simply receive the coin as change from a store? Maybe he didn't know about the SD card at all."

Gabe supposed that was a possibility. "If that's the case, then there's no telling where the passcode is, or if there even is one anymore."

"But that doesn't explain why he was killed." Arnold cracked his knuckles. "I think we need to go on the assumption that Finch did know about the SD card, and that the contents may have led to his death. Either that or something from his past caught up with him. Check and see if he got close to anyone during his time in prison. See if he's gone back there since his release to visit anyone." He turned to look at Gabe. "Do we have anything new on Paige's side of the case?"

"No, sir. Unfortunately, this guy is a ghost. We had evidence that someone was casing her place last night. But the guy's good. Always leaves in a vehicle that he has parked somewhere away from cameras. Wears dark clothing so it's nearly impossible to identify him. And we still can't figure out his motives for going after Paige in the first place."

A fact that continued to frustrate Gabe to no end. If they at least had some idea what he was after, then they could draw the guy out. Anticipate his moves. All they knew right now was that he seemed determined to keep trying.

"Maybe he thinks Finch gave her something when he dropped off the dog? Or hid something nearby?" The suggestion came from Krautscheid. "If he's desperate, there's no telling whether the reasons even make sense or not."

"Could it be the dog?" The moment the words were out, Paris held his hands up. "You know, like she's a witness and might recognize the person who killed Finch. Maybe they want to get a hold of the dog and even get rid of her to make sure that doesn't happen."

Everyone around the table fell silent. Gabe thought that was a stretch, but then again, nothing about this case made much sense. "I suppose that's a possibility."

Arnold seemed to take all their thoughts into consideration. He pointed to Gabe. "I want you to stick with Paige like we discussed. We'll be at the wedding tomorrow, so we can keep an eye out and make sure no one bothers her there, or messes with the wedding. Krautscheid, I'd like for you and Durant to be there as well, dressed in plain clothes. Harrison, what's the plan for the dog?"

"She'll stay with the other vet at the clinic where Paige works. He's agreed to keep her until we can pick her up and get her back to Paige's place." Gabe was glad that it worked out because Paige was worried about leaving the dog at her house alone with stitches.

Arnold nodded. "And I'll keep patrols going both by the clinic as well as Paige's house."

"Sounds good," Paris said. "Meanwhile, I'll keep digging into Finch's financials, talk to his neighbors, and see if I can gather any other clues as to what he was actually involved in. I also located Finch's general practitioner. I'll be going by there today to speak to him about Finch's health and cancer diagnosis. See if Finch ever said something to him that might have raised a red flag."

"I want you to call me if anything major comes up, wedding or no wedding," Arnold instructed.

Agreements sounded around the table.

"All right, let's get back to work."

Even though Gabe wasn't technically on the clock, he helped Paris go through the paperwork they brought back from Finch's house. While he finished up, Paris looked over some more of the financial records that came in about the guy along with details about his past arrests and time in jail.

"He's not exactly swimming in money," he commented. "But he's not completely broke, either. It looks like he had a rough time during his stint in prison though. He had to be hospitalized twice for injuries inflicted by other inmates. Apparently, he didn't get along with anyone else. He was nearly killed once, but a guard caught the fight in action and stepped in, saving his life."

"Maybe that's why it looks like he's been on the straight and narrow since he got out. He doesn't want to go back." Gabe stacked the last of the paperwork and added it to the cardboard box on the floor. "That's it."

"Thanks for your help. You know, you should consider thinking about detective work. You'd be good at it." Paris seemed sincere.

"I appreciate that. But I'm fine right where I'm at." Gabe leaned over and patted Loki who was lying on the floor at his feet. "I can't imagine doing anything else. At least not while this guy is still able to keep on working."

"I can't say as I blame you." Paris reached out and shook Gabe's hand. "If anything else comes to light, I'll be sure to be in touch."

Over the course of the afternoon, Gabe made sure the tuxedos were waiting at the church for the wedding the next day, then he swung by the new house that Bryce and Megan had bought together. Bryce was living there now and then Megan would move in after the wedding.

When Bryce answered the door, he greeted Gabe with a hug. "Good to see you, man. Come on in."

They spent the afternoon going over the rest of the wedding details that Gabe needed to know, and then Bryce entrusted him with the wedding ring.

"Here you go. Keep it safe."

"Of course." He put it in his pocket. "I'm thrilled for you, Bryce. How does it feel to be facing your last night as a single man?"

"Honestly? I'm ready for tomorrow to get here. I mean,

I've wanted to marry Megan for so long. I know she was set on a November wedding, but I would've been fine with a nice, short two-month engagement. Because once you know, you just know." Bryce's face lit up as he talked about Megan and spending the rest of his life with her.

"Yeah, so I've heard." Too bad he felt that way about someone who didn't feel the same in return. "Well, I'd better get going. I need to pick up some fried chicken, then get back to Paige's house before she gets off work. I don't want her walking into a situation where someone's hanging around the place."

"Although if you're going to get there first, it'd be nice if the guy was there waiting."

"Exactly."

"How's Paige doing? Megan said she seemed stressed."

"It's been a rough couple of days." Gabe scratched his chin. "But you know Paige. She's tough. She'll get through this."

"She will. I just hope she knows how lucky she is to have you in her corner." Bryce gave him a knowing look.

"That's what's so great about our group of four. We've all got each other's backs."

A flicker of guilt passed Bryce's features. "We have been so focused on the wedding. I wish we could do more to help you and Paige."

Gabe understood completely. When Megan was threatened last year, he'd been ready to do anything and everything he could to help Megan and Bryce identify the culprit. He also knew Bryce hated that he and Megan were going to be leaving for their honeymoon right in the middle of the current manhunt. "You need to focus on tomorrow, okay? The whole department has us covered. We've got this."

"Yeah, I know you do. But we're here for you guys. Don't forget that."

They said their goodbyes. Gabe got Loki settled in his kennel then went through the drive through for chicken, mashed potatoes, gravy, and rolls. The whole vehicle smelled good, and even Loki rode the rest of the way to Paige's house with his nose pressed up against the mesh separating his kennel from the front seat.

Gabe laughed. "I promise you'll get a bite. But we're waiting for Paige and Lucy to get home first."

He approached the house slowly, taking in the vehicles on the street and any evidence that someone was hanging around the house. Everything seemed to be all clear. He got inside, put the food in the oven to keep it warm, and waited for Paige to get home.

When it was twenty minutes past when he'd expected her, he picked up his phone to call. He thought it was going to voicemail when someone finally answered it and a male voice said, "Hey, Gabe. This is Curtis Whitman."

Dread pooled in Gabe's chest. Curtis was an EMT that Gabe knew through the Search & Rescue team. There was only one reason why Curtis would be answering Paige's phone for her. "Is Paige okay?"

"She's currently stable. I'm transporting her to Destiny Community Hospital momentarily. Here, I'm going to hand Paige's phone to an officer who can give you details."

Gabe grabbed the food out of the oven and shoved it into the fridge. "Thanks, Curtis. I'll be at the hospital as soon as possible."

"You're welcome."

As another voice came over the line, the sound of an ambulance siren filled the air in the background. "Hey, Harrison. It's Blake."

Gabe snapped his fingers for Loki to follow him outside. "Blake. I'm glad you're on the scene. What happened?" He secured Loki in the kennel and climbed behind the steering wheel of his Tahoe.

"Paige was on her way home when someone drove up and shot at her vehicle multiple times. One bullet punctured a tire, causing her to lose control of her car and ultimately crash into a tree."

"Was she hit? All the EMT said was that she was stable." Gabe's grip tightened on his steering wheel until his knuckles went white with the effort. Sounds of a dog barking and snarling came over the phone. "Is that Paige's dog?"

"No, Paige wasn't shot. She was injured, though. I have no more information than that. Yes, the dog's in the back seat of Paige's car and won't let anyone near it. We've got animal control on the way."

"Cancel that call, please. I know the dog. I'll swing by and get her on the way to the hospital."

He got the address from Blake, activated lights and siren, and got there as quickly as he could.

He turned onto Twenty-Seventh Street, and there was no missing the scene. Several police cars were present as well as a fire engine that was getting ready to pull away. Gabe spotted Paige's car on the other side of the shoulder and grimaced. He parked nearby and got out to approach her car. The whole front had caved in around a large tree. He circled the car to see that the front passenger's side tire was flat, and that the window was shattered. Two more bullet holes stood out against the paint on the same side. That likely meant the driver of the other car had been the one to do the shooting.

Gabe's breath came out in a hiss. It was a miracle she

hadn't been killed. In the back, Lucy was a mess of fur and snarls as she bared her teeth at the two officers nearby.

"See, here he is," Blake said to Krautscheid.

Krautscheid turned and frowned. "The dog is traumatized. It's not letting anyone near it. I called for animal control to help get it out safely. Go be with Paige, we've got this."

"It's okay, I know the dog. I think she'll come with me." Gabe crouched low so that his face was even with the window. "Hey, Lucy. It's okay. Good girl."

Lucy stalled. When her tail gave a slight wag, Gabe opened the door a smidgen and put his hand at the crack so that she could smell him. The moment she did, her tail started wagging harder as she licked his hand.

"Good girl. Come on, let's get you out of there." He reached through and grabbed hold of her leash before opening the door completely. Lucy didn't hesitate to go with him.

Gabe turned to Blake and Krautscheid. "Did we catch the guy?"

Blake shook his head. "The vehicle was long gone before we arrived on the scene. But we've got it handled, man. I'll call you regularly with information and updates."

"I appreciate it." He gave them a nod and led Lucy back to his Tahoe. "I'll be at the hospital," he called over his shoulder.

Chapter Nine

If it hadn't been for Gabe's uniform and badge, the nurse outside wouldn't have let him into Paige's room, much less allowed him to bring Lucy along as well. His insistence garnered him several unhappy looks, but Lucy seemed to be on her best behavior.

Gabe softly closed the door behind him. He took in the scene before him. What was it about hospital beds that managed to make everyone look so small and frail? The beeps on the monitor near the bed echoed off the walls in the otherwise silent room. He took a quick glance at the stats on the screen. Her blood pressure and pulse both looked good. An IV entered her left arm at the elbow, held in place by medical tape.

Lucy strained against the leash, and Gabe allowed her to approach the bed. She whined.

"I know, girl, I'm worried about her, too." He reached down and patted the dog's hip.

Still holding onto the leash, Gabe moved to the head of the bed. He laid his hand on Paige's forehead, then carefully brushed some hair away from her eyes. She didn't move a muscle.

A large piece of gauze had been placed on her upper right arm and wrapped with medical tape. He could see some blood starting to seep through.

The door opened again, and a nurse entered the room. "I'm sorry, you can't have that dog in here."

Gabe withdrew his badge and showed it to her. "The dog is related to a case that I'm working on, one that involves Dr. Wade. I'm afraid I was unable to leave her anywhere else."

The nurse, whose name tag read "Nurse Rudd," didn't look convinced, but she said nothing else. "We're going to need to wheel Miss Wade down to imaging to make sure there was no damage to her neck."

"Did something happen to her neck, or is the brace a precaution?"

"I'm afraid only the doctor can answer that question. He'll be in later to check on her."

Gabe resisted the urge to insist that the doctor come in and speak with him now. "What about her arm?"

"Once she's done in imaging, we'll close the wound on her arm." The nurse pointed out the door and to the left. "There's a waiting room down the hall."

"Are you bringing her back here after imaging?"

"Yes."

"Then I'll wait here, thank you." If he could follow them to imaging, he would. Instead, he took a seat in the one extra chair against a wall.

The nurse hesitated a moment before she worked to disconnect Paige from the heart monitor and blood pressure machine before wheeling her bed out of the room.

As soon as she did, the room that seemed tiny before

now looked way too big. The lack of beeps from the monitor were noticeable as well.

Gabe said a silent prayer for Paige's health and for the wisdom of the doctors and nurses tending to her.

His phone rang, and he lifted it to see Bryce's name on the screen. "Hey, I just heard about Paige. Is she okay?"

"She's stable. They took her down to imaging to make sure her neck's okay. She was still unconscious when I got here." That's the part that bothered him the most. If he could have at least spoken to her, then maybe he might feel better about her condition.

"Should I call Megan? We can come down and wait with you."

"No, don't worry about it yet. She's still in the ER, and I doubt they would let you guys in. Let me get an update, and I'll text you soon."

"Alright. Let us know if you need anything."

"Will do. Thanks, man." Gabe hung up. Lucy was watching him as though judging him for allowing the nurse to take Paige in the first place.

Fifteen minutes later, the nurse wheeled Paige's bed back in and hooked her up to the monitor and IV again. "The doctor will be in as soon as possible to update you on the scans and to close her wound." She glanced down at Lucy before leaving.

Gabe scooted his chair closer to Paige and reached for her hand. "You can wake up anytime, Paige. Until you do, I won't be going anywhere." He kissed the back of her hand.

The first thing Paige registered was a splitting headache. Her eyelids lifted a little, but the light around her made the headache worse, and she squeezed them closed again. Where was she? She tried to shift, but something held her legs down.

All at once, everything came flooding back. The car pulling up beside her. The man dressed in black rolling down the window, then shooting at her. The way her car veered off the road. The last thing she remembered was the tree looming in front of her.

"Lucy!" She bolted upright, and immediately a pair of hands cupped her shoulders.

"It's Gabe. I'm right here. Lucy is lying on your legs, and she's fine. You're at the hospital."

Gabe's calm voice washed over her. She allowed herself to lean back against the pillow again before trying to open her eyes. This time, she managed to keep them open despite how much they watered.

Seeing Lucy at the foot of the hospital bed made her feel better, too. "They let you bring her in here?"

"I didn't give them much choice," he said, the tone of his voice serious. "And don't worry, I didn't let her jump up there. I lifted her up. Although there was no stopping her if I hadn't. As long as she's up there with you, she's been sweet to anyone else coming into the room."

"Good girl." She felt the dog's tail thumping against her shins. "My car?"

"Oh, it's a goner. Truly. Although, in my opinion, you were way overdue for something new anyway."

Paige chuckled and then winced against the pain. Still, he wasn't wrong. The poor thing had been falling apart for a while. She sobered as what happened shoved itself into focus. "Gabe, someone shot at me."

"I know." His voice was quiet, yet there was an undertone of anger that was impossible to miss. To her surprise, he leaned over and pressed a kiss to her forehead. "But you are okay." Even when he leaned away, he kept one hand above her pillow just touching her head.

Paige rubbed a thumb against her temple to ease the ache. "How long have I been here?"

"It's been about an hour and a half since they brought you in. I was getting worried that you were asleep for so long." His thumb grazed the top of her head. "Maybe you needed the rest. I was so glad when you finally opened your eyes." He lifted his hand from her pillow and picked up his cell phone. "We're still waiting for the doctor to come back in and let us know how you're doing. I'm also waiting on updates about the crime scene."

"They didn't catch the guy who did it, did they?"

"No. But the good news is, he was sloppy this time. It was in the middle of the day, for one. There's a good chance we'll have caught the vehicle on traffic cameras somewhere. With any luck, they'll recover a bullet, and we can see if it matches any others in the system." There must have been no new messages on his phone because he put it back in his pocket. "I'm seriously angry that this happened to you, but it could lead to a break in the case."

"Silver lining and all." It was about time they got the upper hand.

She shifted to try and get more comfortable, not that Lucy made that easy, only to notice a sharp pain in her upper arm. Paige glanced down at it to find a large bandage covering the area. She groaned. "That's going to look great with my bridesmaid dress tomorrow. Do you think the bandages come in purple?"

Gabe laughed out loud. "Honey, when you walk into the room tomorrow, everyone's going to notice how beautiful you are. The bandage may as well be invisible." As soon as he spoke, the humor faded, and it was clear he meant every word he said.

Paige blinked at him. Between the sweet name and the incredibly nice compliment, she should say something, but motion in the doorway announced the arrival of the doctor.

He glanced at her vitals on the monitor. "Well, Miss Wade, I'd say you are one lucky lady. Scans show no concussion, which is a relief. You're going to be sore for a few days. Your arm got the worst of it thanks to glass from the window. It's a nasty cut, but there's no muscle damage. The nurse will be in to clean it, and then I'll use a few sutures to stitch it closed."

Much like other emergency room experiences Gabe had in the past, things moved rather slowly. He got vehicle insurance information from Paige and spent the time making sure they'd have a rental car dropped off at her house first thing tomorrow morning.

When the nurse came in, it didn't take long for her to clean Paige's wound and then for the doctor to come in and stitch it closed. He finished by placing fresh gauze over it and then wrapping it. He handed her a piece of paper with Wound Care written across the top.

Paige tried to read the print, but her head pounded. "Why does my head hurt so much?"

"You may have some neck strain from the accident."

"Whiplash," said Gabe.

"Exactly. I will prescribe some stronger medication for you since we're heading into the weekend, but you'll want to take acetaminophen every six hours for at least the next day or two. I'll also send in a prescription for a muscle relaxant. In the meantime, get some rest. You can also do some stretches to help your neck." The doctor handed her another paper with a list of exercises.

Then he went on to tell her how often to clean and bandage her arm. He wanted her to see her general practitioner to have the stitches removed in seven to ten days.

He smiled at her. "I'll get the discharge papers signed, then send in a nurse to get you started on a muscle relaxant and remove your IV. You'll be free to go after that. I hope you feel better soon."

"Thank you, doctor." Paige watched him leave.

Gabe stood next to her, a hand on her shoulder. He gave it a squeeze. "Thank God. The minutes between when Curtis told me he was taking you to the hospital and when I saw you in person were some of the longest in my life."

"Curtis?"

"A friend. He's the EMT who responded to your accident." He told her about having to go by the accident scene to pick up Lucy because she wouldn't let anyone else get her out of the car.

Paige chuckled as she looked at the dog who was still lying across her legs. "Good girl, Lucy."

He pointed first to the dog's injury and then Paige's. "And now the two of you match."

"Ha! I guess we do." Suddenly, a thought occurred to her. "Where's Loki?"

"He's in the kennel in my Tahoe. Probably napping away."

"I hope he's not too cold." She felt bad thinking about the poor thing out there by himself.

He pulled a device off his belt. "This will alert me if the inside of the vehicle ever gets too hot or too cold. It's locked, and the heater is running. I also installed a camera in the kennel so I could keep an eye on him." Gabe pulled an application up on his phone, then turned the screen toward her. She could see Loki curled up on the floor of the kennel. He appeared to be fast asleep.

The nurse came in then. "Let's get you out of here, shall we?"

"Yes, please."

A half hour later, she was finally released.

Before going home, Gabe took Paige by the pharmacy to get her medication. By the time that was done, the muscle relaxant she got at the hospital had kicked in completely. It took everything Paige had to stay awake until they got back to her house. She was leaning against the passenger door when Gabe came around to open it.

"Wow, that medication hit you hard, didn't it?"

"Remind me not to take any tomorrow, or I won't be awake for the wedding." She leaned into him as he helped her out of the Tahoe and into her house. He left once she was sitting on the couch and only long enough to bring both dogs back in with him.

He got her a glass of water, set her medications on the kitchen counter, then sat on the coffee table in front of her.

She offered him a tired smile. "I'm fine, Gabe. I need to go get some sleep. Any updates from the station?"

"I got a text from Paris. They recovered two bullets and are in the process of comparing them to any others in the system. They are also combing through footage from traffic light cameras in the area and contacting any homes or businesses there to see if we can get the car on camera. We should hear more tomorrow."

"I don't want anything to mess up Bryce and Megan's wedding." She got her phone and checked the weather app. "Did you see we're expecting another winter storm tomorrow night? It's a good thing their wedding is early in the afternoon. Hopefully, they can get on the plane for their honeymoon before it hits."

"I still can't believe we're having this much winter weather in November." Gabe scowled.

"Maybe this will fill our quota until next winter." Paige covered a yawn. "I'm going to go to bed before I can't walk straight." She thought about his compliment at the hospital again for the hundredth time. "What you said earlier..."

He appeared to immediately know what she was referring to. It was scary how often that seemed to be happening lately. "I meant every word. You are the most beautiful woman I've ever known. It's one of the first things I noticed when we met. I couldn't believe a girl like you would even take the time to talk to a guy like me back then." He laughed. Then he reached over and gently swept some hair away from her face. "I'm so glad you did, though."

Paige's breath hitched. Clearly these meds were making her loopy because she had to stop herself from reaching for him. For a moment, she considered what it would be like to kiss him. To be held by him. "I'm glad we met, too," she said, the words sounding rushed even to her. "I'd better go get some sleep, or I won't be worth much tomorrow." She stood slowly, and it felt like every muscle in her body protested.

Gabe rose, a confused expression on his face. Before she allowed herself to overthink it, she leaned in and placed a light kiss on his cheek. "Thank you. For everything."

Lucy followed her out of the living room and to Paige's room. Despite the tremulous thoughts going through her head, Paige barely managed to make it to the bed before sleep overtook her.

Gabe had no idea whether he should regret blurting what he thought to Paige or not. He was even more confused by her reaction. At first, she seemed surprised. Upset, even. But then she'd kissed him on the cheek. It wasn't anything noteworthy, except that in all the years he'd known her, she'd never done that before.

It might have given him hope if it weren't for the fact that she was so exhausted between the accident and the medication. Would she even remember their conversation in the morning?

Things were changing between them. They were subtle, maybe, but they were there all the same. What that meant, though, Gabe didn't know. Even if it only led to seeing Paige more often when all of this was over, he'd take it.

It was well after eleven, but Gabe still felt too wound up to sleep after such a crazy day. Why had the person fired at Paige's vehicle and not simply waited to shoot her instead? Or was there a purpose behind it? If he was trying to scare Paige, then he'd accomplished that.

Gabe found some ham in the fridge and made himself a sandwich. At least they could eat the fried chicken tomorrow.

He hadn't heard a single sound from Paige's room, even though he could see light through the space beneath the door. Had she gone right to sleep? Surely, she had, but he couldn't erase an image of her collapsed on the floor from of his mind.

He finally decided it would be best to at least peek in and make sure she was okay. He twisted the doorknob and eased it open enough to step through, telling Loki to stay outside. Paige's still form was on the bed, and Gabe immediately breathed a sigh of relief.

Lucy was lying on the floor between the bed and the door. Her head popped up. She looked at him, then wagged her tail.

"Good girl. I'm glad you're watching over her," he whispered as he patted her head. That's when he noticed that Paige was still dressed and hadn't even taken her shoes off. The room held a chill, too, and she was sleeping on top of the covers. Judging by the way her body was curled, she was probably cold even if she didn't realize it.

Gently, he removed her shoes and set them on the floor.

Paige shifted and raised her head. "Is everything okay?"

"Everything's fine. You fell asleep with your shoes on. It's going to be cold tonight. You should get under the covers."

When she got up from the bed, she seemed a little unsteady, so he put an arm around her until she pulled the covers back and climbed underneath. He tugged them up over her shoulders, taking care not to bump her injured arm.

Gabe thought she'd fallen right back to sleep again and was ready to take his leave when she spoke from behind him.

"It's too cold to sleep on the floor."

"What?"

She turned just enough to look at him. "It's too cold for you to sleep on the floor. Share the bed. There are blankets in the hall closet." With that, she rolled back over and was breathing deeply in moments.

Gabe simply stared at her. He had to admit he wasn't looking forward to another night on the floor. And there would be more than enough room on her queen-sized bed. Still, he wasn't sure he should until he thought about her injuries and how disoriented the muscle relaxants had made her.

He decided he'd rather play it safe and stay nearby in case she needed anything. He'd sleep on top of the covers. He was also an early riser, so he'd likely be awake before her.

Happy with his decision, Gabe made sure all the doors were locked, found the blankets in the closet, and then left the light on in the living room before going back to the bedroom. Paige hadn't moved a muscle since he left.

Loki followed him in and immediately found a spot on the floor to lie down. He seemed settled so Gabe took his shoes off and eased himself onto the other side of the bed so as not to disturb Paige. He pulled the heavy blanket over himself.

Considering how busy the day had been, he thought it might be difficult to fall asleep. The next thing he knew, it was two in the morning, and Paige was sitting up in bed.

"Are you okay?" he asked.

"Just running to the bathroom." She groaned as she stood. "I feel like I was hit by a truck."

That had his attention. "Are you dizzy?" He got off the bed in case she needed help.

"No, but I am sore. I'll be right back."

Gabe checked his phone for messages until she returned.

She eased into bed again. "Sorry I woke you."

"It's okay. Get some more rest."

"Thanks for staying in here, Gabe. I feel a lot safer." Moments later, her breathing evened off, and she was asleep again.

"You're welcome," he replied, even though he doubted she heard him. Loki walked over and nudged his hand for a pat before lying on the floor right by Gabe's side of the bed.

"God, please help Paige's wounds to heal quickly and

completely," he whispered. "Please give me and the rest of those protecting Paige the wisdom to know what to do. Keep us all safe tomorrow. Thank you for your mercies."

He easily could have lost Paige today. It was the second time this week that her life had been endangered. It was becoming a theme, and Gabe had had enough.

Chapter Ten

When Paige woke the next morning, it took a few extra moments to clear the cobwebs from her head. She remembered coming home from the hospital and talking to Gabe, but it was almost like watching a scene through a hazy fog. She'd never had muscle relaxants before, and she prayed she'd never have to take another one.

The memory of kissing Gabe on the cheek came to mind, and she groaned. A glance at the other side of the bed revealed an extra blanket where she knew Gabe had slept last night.

How was it possible to feel so safe and so uncertain all at the same time?

On one hand, knowing he was there to watch over her and help her if she needed it made her feel protected. Special.

But it also scared her because she found herself wondering what it'd be like to wake up next to someone every morning. Then her thoughts quickly shifted from an unnamed "someone" to Gabe specifically.

That wasn't in the cards. Never had been. But kissing his cheek last night... She could still feel the way the stubble had lightly scratched her lips. Yeah, that was a huge mistake. One she had no idea what to do about. Pretend it never happened?

That's when she heard voices coming from the kitchen. She got ready for the day, then left her room to find Gabe talking to Chief Dolman along with Detective Paris.

"Good morning," she greeted them, glad she'd made herself presentable before leaving her room.

The chief nodded toward her arm. "Good morning. How are you feeling today?"

"Honestly?" Paige lifted her shoulders and rolled her head, her neck twinging in response. "I'm sore, but I think taking the muscle relaxant was worse. I do not like feeling that loopy."

"I'm not a fan of them, either," Detective Paris said. "I hope you don't mind that we dropped by. We figured we could update you both on the case."

The chief took a sip of his coffee. "Which meant we may as well bring breakfast while we were at it." He grabbed a bag and dumped out a half dozen breakfast burritos along with packets of salsa. "Help yourself. We got you a coffee, too."

"You gentlemen are welcome to stop by anytime. Thank you so much." Paige could certainly use the caffeine. She grabbed a burrito and sat down in the empty chair across the table from the chief. Gabe and Detective Paris ate while leaning against the counter.

Detective Paris finished a bite of his burrito before he began. "Ballistics came back with nothing—there was no match between the bullets pulled from your car and anything in the system."

Paige tried to stifle her disappointment. She'd hoped this might lead to the person who'd tried to kill her, or at least point the way toward who or what he was affiliated with. Something besides this constant guesswork that was getting them nowhere.

As though he could sense her troubled thoughts, Gabe moved away from the counter to stand behind her chair and place a protective hand on her shoulder. "What about the suspect's car?"

"A traffic camera got a visual on the vehicle that forced you off the road." Paris pulled a photo out of a large envelope and showed it to them. "No good pictures of his face. The car was stolen, and we only know that because we found it early this morning after someone left it on some private property and torched it. There seems to be no connection between that and the owners of the property."

Gabe frowned. "Which means we're no closer to figuring out who this person is."

"Maybe," the chief said. "But we've got a little more background info on Finch." He motioned to Detective Paris to continue.

"I spoke with his doctor, and it seems that Finch did know about his cancer diagnosis. However, his insurance left a lot to be desired, and he couldn't afford treatment. Maybe his need for money led him to seek out a way to make a large amount of it, and quickly. But that's all just conjecture, since we don't have any solid proof." He took another large bite of his breakfast burrito.

"Then I take it his financials weren't much help?" Gabe wadded up his empty wrapper.

"Only to show the guy was completely average. There were no large deposits or any activity that raised a red flag." The detective set his burrito down. "I did talk to his neighbors and discovered that no one really knew him. They said he was quiet and kept to himself. They did remember his dog, but get this: two different neighbors said he only got her last week."

Gabe threw his trash away. "Hold on. I grabbed some of her things from Finch's house yesterday. What with the shooting and all, I never did bring them in. I'll go get them."

Paige told the other officers about how she thought Lucy's collar and leash looked brand new. "Maybe that's why she doesn't have a rabies tag or license, too. Finch never had the chance to get one."

Gabe returned and set a large garbage bag on the ground. He reached in and pulled out a dog bed, which he shook out and set down. Lucy walked over and curled up on it. He also withdrew a set of food and water bowls and three toys which he placed on the counter. "They do all look new," he acknowledged.

Paige's gaze went to Lucy who was watching Gabe with an eagle eye, probably wishing he'd give her the toys. "None of this makes any sense."

"Maybe he needed the dog as a prop of sorts. You know, to look the part of a jogger in the park in order to pass off the SD card." The suggestion came from Gabe, who had moved back to lean against the counter, but he didn't look convinced.

Paige motioned to Lucy. "Then where did Finch get her? She's obviously in good health and has been well taken care of. If he was running from someone, he cared enough about her to bring her by the clinic instead of leaving her to die." As far as she was concerned, that meant he couldn't have been all bad.

"I'll put in a call to the rescue groups in town as well as

animal control. Maybe she was adopted from one of them," Paris said.

"We may never know where she came from, or why she was in Finch's possession," Chief Dolman concluded. "It's possible these people may think Finch gave you the SD card, Paige. Or that the SD card is hidden somewhere on Lucy. Maybe they think Finch put it in her collar or something similar."

"So they're going to keep coming after me until they're convinced that I don't have what they're looking for?" The idea was terrifying. "Lucy has been through a lot, and who knows what happened to her before she ended up with Finch. I'm not going to send her somewhere else." Besides, if the focus were on Lucy, she wasn't about to potentially send a problem on to someone else.

"That's not necessary," the chief insisted. "I'm going to have an officer at the vet clinic today since Lucy will be there, then we'll bump up patrols both there and at your house. Whoever is behind this is going to slip up soon, and when he does, we're going to be there to catch him." He stood and everyone else followed suit. "We'll get out of your hair. I know you've got a lot to do to get ready before the wedding. Chloe's waiting for me at home, too. I'll see you both at the church in a few hours."

"Yes, sir," Gabe said and then shook his hand. He shook Paris's as well. "Thanks for stopping by, we appreciate it."

Paige and Gabe saw them to the door just as an insurance agent was walking up to the house. There were two cars parked out front—one was Paige's rental and the other was driven by a second agent waiting to take the first back to the office.

They got everything squared away. Paige pocketed the keys, and then they went back inside and closed and locked the door behind them. Already exhausted, she sighed and leaned against the door. It was hard not to be discouraged.

"Hey," Gabe stopped in front of her. "We've got this."

"I know." She ran her hands over her face. "And to think, only a few days ago, my primary complaint was the snow. I'd happily go back to that." She chuckled, then looked at her watch. "We need to get a move on. They're expecting us at the church in about an hour." At least they wouldn't have to worry about changing now since her dress and his suit were at the church.

Paige pushed away from the door and went to clean up after breakfast. She bent to pick something up, and her neck twinged. She jolted to a stop and winced.

"I'll take care of this. What else do you need to do before we go?" Gabe finished picking up the rest of the trash and throwing it away, then wiped off the table.

She still needed to clean her cut and redress it. She considered managing the whole thing herself but lifted her arm instead. "Could you help me get this bandage off? The angle makes it difficult for me to see. I can handle the rest after that." She imagined a nasty, jagged cut underneath that the tape might be stuck to.

Gabe looked surprised. "Of course, I'll help." He washed and dried his hands. She held her arm out, and he carefully rolled her sleeve up until the white tape was visible. "Okay, let's see if we can get this old bandage off." Slowly, he peeled the tape away from her skin until he was able to lift the bandage, revealing the cut beneath it. Gabe ran a thumb lightly against her skin near the wound and whistled. "I think it's going to leave quite a scar."

Paige made a point to ignore the way his touch sent goosebumps down her arm. She craned her neck to try and get a good look at it, but the muscles protested. "At least it's not in too bad of a spot. I can cover it up with long sleeves, or show it off if I need an interesting story to break the ice."

Her comment earned her a deep laugh. "You are something else. At least you can go in and have the stitches removed in a week or two. I think the worst part is when it starts to heal, and the stitches get itchy."

"I was planning to take them out myself. It'd be a lot easier. But I don't think I'll be able to reach."

Gabe looked so surprised that Paige had to laugh. "I remove stitches all the time from dogs and cats who squirm, try to jump off the table, or growl and hiss at me. Trust me, this would be a breeze."

"Yeah, I suppose it would, then." He shook his head in wonder. "If only the kids back in high school could see you now. I guarantee the guys would've been lining up to ask you to prom."

"I highly doubt that." They both knew she'd been more of a tomboy back then. Besides, for a long time, she'd held onto a secret hope that Gabe might look at her as more than a friend. She'd never been interested in anyone else. The memory sent heat to her cheeks. "I'll clean this up, slap a new bandage on, and we can get going. Reg will be at the clinic waiting for us."

"You can't even see it, much less reach it. Let me help."

She wanted to refuse, but he was right. Cleaning it herself would be awkward at best. "I appreciate it." They moved to the bathroom where Paige had left all the supplies. She watched him in the mirror as he set about cleaning the area. "You mentioned stitches being itchy. When did you have stitches?"

He paused, his hands hovering just above her skin. It was clear he was reluctant to tell her.

"Spit it out, Harrison." Even before he spoke, she knew

it must have been while he was on duty, and that's why he hesitated to say anything.

Gabe tossed the alcohol wipe in the trash. He lifted his shirt enough to show her a white scar near his ribs. "A suspect had a knife I didn't see. Thankfully, he was apprehended seconds after this."

She turned and, as though her hand had a mind of its own, ran a finger over the scar. Even though it was short, she could feel the thick scar tissue below the skin. With a start, she pulled her hand back and turned around again. "I'm glad you're okay."

"Me, too."

The air between them practically sparked with energy. Paige swallowed and tried not to notice as he lowered his shirt and reached for the antibiotic ointment. He slathered some on her cut then covered it with fresh gauze. "Do you want me to tape it on like before? Or wrap it with one of these stretchy bandages?"

"Let's go with wrapping it. I think it's more likely to stay for the duration of the day."

"Sounds good." He deftly wrapped her wound without getting it too tight. "How's that?"

"That's perfect." Paige looked at their reflections in the bathroom mirror. Gabe started to pack the extra supplies in a small bag.

"We should take these in case you need them." He looked up and met her eyes in the mirror. He lifted the bottle of Tylenol. "Have you taken any yet?"

She shook her head and turned to face him again.

He opened the bottle, shook two tablets out, and handed them to her. As Gabe placed the medication in the palm of her hand, he covered hers with his own. "Keep up on the meds today, okay? I don't want you to end up hurting."

"Yeah, okay." Paige took in a slow breath, fully aware of how close they were standing. She needed to take a step back, pull her hand away, something.

Gabe's gaze darted to her lips and back to her eyes as he shifted closer.

Paige moved her hand from his, but it took more effort than she liked to admit. "I'll go get a glass of water so I can take these."

She retreated to the kitchen. After swallowing the medication, she leaned against the counter with a sigh. Gabe had nearly kissed her, and she'd nearly let him.

"Get ahold of yourself," she said under her breath.

They had a wedding to focus on and best friends to support.

All while trying to keep a crazy person from messing anything up.

The last thing she needed to do was complicate it with her confusing feelings toward Gabe. When all of this was over, they'd go back to the way things were before.

They were friends.

Always had been.

Always would be.

Chapter Eleven

Ever since they left Paige's house, Gabe noticed she'd been more quiet than normal. Especially after they had dropped the dogs off at the clinic. "They're going to be fine."

"I know." She glanced at him.

"Everything is under control. I know it's easier said than done, but try not to worry. Officer Durant is going to be sticking close to you. I promise I'll never be that far away. If you need something, all you have to do is call or text me." He grinned at her. "You could probably holler, but that might be a little disruptive." He hoped his joke might make her smile.

Paige chuckled. "I can see the headline now: Bridesmaid Scares Ever-living Daylights out of the Bride on Wedding Day. Yeah, let's avoid that if we can."

Gabe was glad he could lighten her mood. A part of him wondered if their closeness that morning had freaked her out. He'd been three seconds away from kissing her when she'd left for the kitchen. There was no way she hadn't guessed his intentions, which meant she purposefully avoided the kiss.

Then again, considering everything she'd been through over the last few days, whatever was happening between them was probably a negligible blip on her map of concerns. He tried to ignore the twinge of disappointment at the thought.

The First Church of the Nazarene came into view. He found a parking spot and took in the gray sky. "It looks like winter weather is coming, doesn't it?"

Paige eyed the sky with a frown. "Smells like it, too. I kept hoping they were wrong about more snow. With any luck, it'll hold off for a while still."

He hoped so, too. There were a dozen cars in the parking lot as people worked tirelessly to get everything ready for the wedding. No doubt Megan and Bryce were already here, too.

They walked into the building together to find Durant waiting for them. Gabe made the introductions. "Paige, this is Officer Jenny Durant. Durant, this is Paige Wade."

The women shook hands.

"I appreciate you staying close by," Paige said sincerely.

"My pleasure," Durant said with a smile.

Someone stopped by and swept Paige away to help the bride get ready. Durant was right behind them. Paige glanced over her shoulder at Gabe before she disappeared around the corner.

"You'll see her again later," Bryce teased as he entered the hall. He must have gotten there just in time to see them arrive.

"Funny." He motioned to his best friend's suit. "You clean up good there, Keyes. Looks like you're ready to get hitched or something."

"So ready. Come on, you can come help me with a few things and update me on Paige's case."

Gabe told his buddy about the latest information and how Paige was doing after the shooting yesterday. "She's tough, man. But I can tell she's exhausted. I want to catch this guy, so she can go back to her life. Feel safe again, you know?"

"I know. And what are you going to do when this is all over?"

"You mean, what am I going to do about Paige and me?" There was no use pretending that Bryce meant anything else. "I don't know. I value her friendship, and the idea of jeopardizing that bothers me. But I'm not sure I can keep moving forward without being honest about how I feel. If something happened to her, I'd regret that for the rest of my life."

Gabe knew his friend had gone through something similar with Megan last year. It'd worked out for them. He could only pray that there was some future together for him and Paige, too.

"Megan and I are both praying for you guys. Just know that, no matter what, you'll both still have us. That won't change. We'll figure it out."

"I appreciate it."

Bryce's dad came into the room. "Guests are starting to arrive, son. You'd better let me help you with that tie."

Gabe clapped his buddy on the shoulder. "I'm going to check in with Arnold and make sure Paige is doing okay. I'll be back in a sec."

Bryce gave him a nod, then lifted his chin so that his dad could fix his tie.

The church was bustling with activity as guests came in and were seated. Gabe spotted Krautscheid at the end of the hall, dressed to blend in with everyone else, and headed that way. "Have you seen the chief?"

Krautscheid pointed. "He and the wife went that way." He held out an earpiece. "This is for you."

"Thanks." He placed it in his ear. When he first started at the academy, it'd taken a while to get used to having so many different voices coming through his earpiece. Couple that with a loud environment or a second radio, and it was a lot. Now, sifting through all the sounds around him came as second nature. "I'm going to find Paige to make sure she's okay, then get back to the groom."

He found Arnold in the sanctuary along with his wife, Chloe. It'd only been a little over a year and a half since Gabe had attended their wedding. He shook Arnold's hand, then gave Chloe a smile. "It's great to see you."

Chloe smiled brightly as she tucked some of her blonde hair behind one ear and put a hand in the crook of her husband's elbow. "Thank you, Gabe. It's good to see you." She glanced at Arnold. "We are hoping to host a holiday party sometime in the first half of December. We'd love for you to come."

"That sounds like fun, thank you."

Arnold put an arm around Chloe. "We'll be sure to narrow down the date before too long. It always seems like, once November arrives, the holidays get here before we know it."

"That it does." Gabe scanned the room but didn't see the woman he was looking for. "Have either of you bumped into Paige?"

Arnold shook his head.

Chloe motioned toward one of the back doors. "She's probably in with Megan." She gave him directions to the changing room the bride was using. "Just make sure you knock first," she said with a laugh.

"Wise advice." Gabe wound his way through the growing number of guests and easily found the changing room Chloe told him about. He rapped on the door with the back of his hand. "Paige? Are you in there?"

Giggling women's voices answered his call before the door opened wide enough for Paige to slip through.

Every thought in his head evaporated as he took in the floor-length teal dress that hung from her frame as though it'd been made for her alone. Fabric gathered at the front to accentuate her curves. The dress had short sleeves with lace the same color that partially covered the bandage on her arm.

Paige had left her hair down to fall past her shoulders to the middle of her back.

When he finally focused, he found her dark eyes watching his face as she bit her lip nervously. "I know. This is so not me, although I think the color is pretty." She put a hand over the bandage as though she were trying to hide it.

"Are you kidding?" He reached for that hand and gently pulled it away from her arm, twirling her once in the process. "You look positively gorgeous."

Paige had been so nervous about wearing the dress that hearing Gabe's words was like diving into the ocean. His compliment stole her breath while it simultaneously cooled her nerves. It didn't matter how many times Megan had told her the dress looked beautiful on her; it was completely different when Gabe said the same thing.

But then, just like the ocean, there was that sneaky

undercurrent. The one hiding right below the surface threatening to take everything she thought she knew and yank it all away.

Because right now, Gabe's opinion of her meant way more to her than it should. She withdrew her hand from his and worked to smooth out the skirt of the dress, even though the fabric was practically flawless, to buy herself a moment.

"Thank you," she said, her voice barely above a whisper. Not only did his suit make him look like someone straight out of a James Bond movie, but the handkerchief folded and placed in the breast pocket was the same shade of teal as her dress. "You might consider wearing suits more yourself. It's not a bad look on you."

He laughed out loud at her comment and bowed slightly. "Thank you, ma'am, but I'm afraid suits are reserved for weddings and funerals." He used one finger to slightly loosen the collar. "Ties are evil. I'm just saying."

"As are dress shoes," she agreed. She lifted the skirt of her dress enough to hold a foot out to showcase the platform shoes she was wearing. Although, as far as dress shoes went, they could've been a whole lot worse. At least they were pretty, and they didn't have heels. "How's everything going out here?" Paige had been wondering if there was any news, and a change in subject was a plus.

"We're good. Everything is going according to plan, and there's no sign of trouble. Bryce is ready and chomping at the bit. I wanted to check with you before the ceremony begins. How's Megan? Is Officer Durant in with you ladies?"

"Megan looks beautiful. She's ready to go, too. Yes, and Jenny is so nice. Apparently, she has five older sisters that are all married, so she knows all the little tips and tricks to keep everything on track." That was no exaggeration, either. Jenny had managed to single-handedly solve two minor issues with the dress not a half-hour after arriving.

"I'm glad to hear that." He checked his watch, then paused with one finger near his ear. When he turned his head, she spotted the earpiece nestled there. "Okay, I need to head back. I'll see you in there?"

"I'll see you there." She waited until he'd rounded a bend in the hallway before going back inside.

"Who was that?" Megan asked as she looked at Paige in the mirror she was standing in front of.

"Gabe. He wanted to let me know that we are all good to go." Paige stood with her hands on her hips. "I think I speak for everyone here when I say you are officially the most beautiful bride-to-be I have ever seen."

Events moved quickly from there, and before Paige knew it, she was standing at the front of the church listening as Megan and Bryce said their vows.

Movies and commercials made it sound like all couples encountered prewedding jitters or got cold feet at some point during the engagement. That wasn't true for these two. Paige never knew them to be anything but excited to marry each other.

And that's exactly what she wanted some day. To meet and fall in love with a man that she couldn't wait to spend the rest of her life with.

She spared a quick glance at Gabe only to find he'd been watching her, too. He gave her a wink then returned his attention to the ceremony, effectively setting a whole swarm of butterflies fluttering in her stomach.

When the couple shared their first official kiss as husband and wife, it took everything in Paige to blink back the happy tears. They turned and walked back down the aisle with their arms around each other as their friends and family cheered.

Gabe stopped in front of Paige and held his elbow toward her. "Can I escort you, my lady?"

She dipped her chin in acceptance as she slid her hand into the crook of his elbow. "They did it," she breathed.

"Yep. And so did you. Not even a stumble."

Paige forgot all about their conversation the other day and laughed. "And I see you didn't misplace the ring. All in all, it was quite a success."

"They are insanely sweet together. It's almost sickening." Even though Paige spoke the words, a happy smile lit up her face as she turned toward Gabe. "I'm happy for them. You know?"

"Yeah, me, too."

Gabe took a taste of his champagne. He'd never been a fan of the stuff. The few sips he'd had today would last him years. He gazed at Paige across the small table. Her attention followed Bryce and Megan as they seemed to float over the dance floor for their first dance together as husband and wife. Paige did look happy, but there was something else there too. Wistfulness, maybe?

If so, he could certainly sympathize. It's not like he'd ever thought much about what his own wedding might look like. That wasn't really a guy thing to do. But wondering what it would be like to have someone to come home to? To grow old with? Oh yeah, he'd thought about that often.

There was no denying that Paige's face was always the one he saw, too. For years, he'd done everything he could to give her space. Make sure he never crossed that line to make her uncomfortable or disrespect her decision to not marry someone in law enforcement.

Paige hadn't dated often through the years—or at least not that he knew of. But the few times he saw her with someone else had been painful. Did she feel the same way when he'd dated other women in the past?

It seemed as though they were never meant to be together.

But tonight ... he wanted tonight to be different. Even if it was just for Bryce and Megan's wedding.

The guests were invited onto the floor to dance. Gabe immediately stood and extended a hand to Paige. "Will you do me the honor?"

Her dark eyes widened, and her pretty mouth opened in surprise. "Gabe, I'm not sure it's such a good idea."

"Why not?"

If she truly had no feelings for him, then this wouldn't be a big deal. Right?

Doubt marched across her features followed by a stubborn tilt of her chin.

Before she could shoot him down flat, he motioned to the dance floor. "I'm the best man, and you're the maid of honor. I think one dance together is expected." He was no expert on weddings, but that was one thing he was pretty sure of.

He must have been right because Paige's resolve melted. She stood from the chair, careful to arrange the skirt around her, and softly placed her hand in his. "One dance."

He'd take it. He escorted her onto the dance floor, placed one arm around her waist, and cradled her hand in his. The scent of her shampoo danced with the fragrance of the flowers that decorated the indoor space around them.

Gabe doubted he'd ever be able to forget that combination for as long as he lived.

The slow song drew them into its melody as Gabe held her close. She flowed to the music. Being with her like this was easy. Natural. As though she were meant to be in his arms. "You're a beautiful dancer," he whispered, his mouth not far from her ear.

Paige ducked her head a little. "Thank you. I took lessons before our senior prom."

"And then you never went." She was supposed to go—they were supposed to meet there as friends. Bryce and Megan were a couple back then, and without Paige there, Gabe had felt like a third wheel.

He'd been upset to learn she'd chosen to stay home. Until he found out she and her family had gotten the news that her brother was killed overseas. A month later, her uncle, who served on the police force in California, had been killed in the line of duty.

It wasn't long afterward that Paige declared she would never fall for a man who served like her brother or uncle did. That she wasn't going to put herself in a position to lose someone she loved like that.

He still remembered the day he signed up for the police academy. He hadn't told Paige yet until it was official. He'd never forget the disappointment and anger in her eyes when she found out.

Of course, their friendship endured. But the closeness they once had seemed to fade. He'd missed it. And even though a horrible set of events had brought them together again this last week, he'd enjoyed spending more time with her.

He watched her now, concerned by the shadow of sadness in her eyes.

"Hey, are you okay? Is this bringing back too many memories?"

"Maybe. It's making me think about my brother, but only because it reminds me of where I would've been that night if he hadn't died." She kept her gaze glued to his tie. "You know me. I don't go for fancy. This is probably the first dress I've worn since Tommy's funeral." She swallowed. "I took dance lessons so I wouldn't make a fool of myself in front of you at prom."

Gabe's eyebrows rose to meet his hairline. She'd taken dance lessons specifically so she could dance with him at their prom? That was news to him. "I already knew how to dance. But it took some doing to build up the courage to ask you to dance with me. I'd like to think I wouldn't have chickened out."

Paige's chin rose until her eyes met his. "I would've agreed to the dance. Back then."

She left something unspoken, but Gabe heard it as clearly as the music floating around them.

Before her brother died.

Before her uncle was killed.

Before she decided she wasn't going to put herself in a position to worry about a loved one's safety every single day.

"I've missed you, Paige." It felt as though his heart was beating right out of his chest.

"Gabe, I'm sorry. I'm sorry I took a step back in our friendship. I'm sorry if you felt like I didn't care anymore. It wasn't that." She looked away from him. "If anything, it was the opposite."

He'd once suspected as much. No, they never verbally expressed an interest in each other. But he'd had no doubt back then that his feelings for her were reciprocated at least to some degree.

"So you figured, by taking a step back, you could protect yourself. Make sure you didn't end up like your aunt or your mom, having to bury a loved one killed in the line of duty. If you could stop caring, it would be easier."

"Is that such a bad reason?" One tear gathered in the corner of her eye and spilled over onto her cheek.

"No, it's not," he said, his voice soft. "But let me ask you one question: did it help?"

Paige sniffed, frustrated with herself for crying at Megan's reception. And even more upset that she was crying in front of Gabe while being held in his arms. As he'd escorted her onto the dance floor, she'd clung to her resolve to get through the dance as gracefully as possible. But the moment his arms went around her? All of that melted away.

This was Gabe. Not the police officer or even the kid she used to go to school with. This was the man that she'd convinced herself she could avoid falling in love with if she put enough space and time between them.

Did taking a step back help?

Not even a little, because even after all these years, how she felt about him never waned. Grew, changed, and shifted, yes. But it'd never gone away.

She gave a slight shake of her head in answer to his question. She wasn't even sure he'd seen it until he swept some of the hair from her cheek and deposited it behind her ear. "Look at me, Paige."

She squeezed her eyes shut, willing herself to keep her emotions in check. But the moment she opened them again and found him watching her, his smile tender and eyes full of understanding, she sucked in a breath of air. Emotion slammed into her chest, her heart skipping a beat.

"Me, either," he said, his voice scarcely above a whisper. "I was so in love with you."

She'd suspected. Feared that was the case. Because she'd been falling, too. Which was why, when he'd announced he was joining the police academy, she knew that things between them would never work out.

So why couldn't her heart accept that and move on?

"I was in love with you, too." More tears gathered in her eyes, and she desperately blinked them away.

"What about now?" The words came on a breath that brushed her cheek.

"Why does it matter, Gabe? Your job hasn't changed. My fears—and I admit that's exactly what they are—haven't changed, either. So why does it matter how I do or don't feel?"

"Because it matters to me. And Paige, you can try all you want to convince yourself otherwise, but I think it does to you, too." Gabe shook his head, clearly frustrated. "Don't you think I would've moved on if I could? God knows I've tried. You have no idea how many times I prayed that these feelings for you would disappear." He took a slight misstep as he guided her on the dance floor but corrected himself.

"So did I." Her words were barely above a whisper, but they drew him in. "I'm scared, Gabe. I'm scared because I'm not sure which is worse right now. To go on feeling this way and pretending differently. Or to put myself in a position where, *every day*, I would worry about whether you're going to come home." Her voice cracked.

He paused. "Can I ask you a question?" She gave a slight nod in response. "Have you talked to your mom and aunt? I know their losses were huge. I can't even begin to imagine what they went through. But if you were to ask them, do you think they'd tell you they have regrets?"

That snagged her attention. "What do you mean?"

"Do you think your aunt regrets falling in love and marrying your uncle? Do you think she'd choose to do the same all over again even knowing what happened to him? I'm willing to bet she never regretted a thing. And your mom ... I know she treasures every minute she had with your brother. Think about everything they missed out on in life. The love. The memories." His voice was kind, the expression in his eyes soft and caring.

"No. Neither would have changed a thing about their lives before that moment." She didn't hesitate because she knew that was true. Even still, she couldn't shake the memories of how her mom spent months in mourning, crying, eventually choosing to move away so that she didn't have constant memories of her son surrounding her. If it hadn't been for the fact that her parents had each other and their faith in God, Paige didn't know what would've happened. Her aunt didn't fare as well. She'd turned to drinking to drown her sorrows. She was sober now, but it'd taken years to get to that point.

Losing their loved ones nearly destroyed them. Paige couldn't even allow herself to imagine someone knocking on her door to let her know that Gabe would never be coming home again.

Panic cinched like a vice against her ribcage. "I can't do this, Gabe. Not here." Because no matter which way this went, she was going to end up a blubbery mess. She refused to allow that to happen on her best friend's special day.

As if on cue, the music stopped, and everything in the room shifted into focus. Paige nearly tripped as she took a giant step away from Gabe then felt horrible as a flash of disappointment crossed his features. "I need something to drink."

Without waiting, she spun on her heels and headed for the refreshment table on the far side of the room.

It had been stupid to agree to dance with him. Stupid to let herself think about Gabe in any way outside of friendship.

She reached for the first non-alcoholic drink she could find and cupped the cool glass in her hands. Willed it to ground her. She took a sip before she allowed herself to scan the small crowd to see where Gabe had gone.

She spotted him not far from where she'd left him. He was talking to Bryce, a grin on his face as he shook the groom's hand. But even in the exchange, Gabe glanced at her, a hint of concern in his eyes.

Paige didn't have to worry about what to do next, because Megan found her then and pulled her to the side.

"I'm sorry that Bryce and I are leaving when the case is still open. We could postpone the honeymoon. Wait until spring."

"Don't you dare." Paige reached for her best friend and gave her a hug. "You and Bryce deserve this. Besides, we're expecting that winter storm to hit tonight. Why on earth would you choose to stay here for that when you could be lounging on the beach somewhere?" Paige squeezed Megan's hand. "Get out of here. Be happy. I'll see you in a week."

Megan's eyes shone with tears as she smiled. "Thanks. I love you, my sweet friend."

"I love you, too. Now go find that groom of yours."

The women laughed over one more hug, and then Paige watched her friend walk away, a vision in white.

A short time later, the guests cheered and waved as the

limousine pulled away. Immediately, the atmosphere shifted. Some of the guests continued to dance or enjoy the snack foods, but many of them started to leave.

Paige stood on the sidewalk, her arms wrapped around her middle, and stared at the street where the limousine had been just minutes before.

That's when she felt, more than saw, Gabe approach. He stopped several feet away, hands tucked into his pockets. "You okay?"

"I'm super happy for them. I guess I'm just realizing how different things are going to be now, you know? Not that it's bad. Just..."

"Different. Yeah, I get what you mean. Change is scary."

The weight of that last sentence hung between them. He was talking about more than the wedding and their small social circle, and they both knew it.

He paused for several moments. "Are you ready to leave? I can take you home. Or we can stay. Whichever you prefer."

"No, I don't want to stay." She glanced around them and shook her head. "We should probably change first. How about I meet you here in about twenty minutes?"

She got dressed quickly, leaving her gown hanging on a small rack in the hallway. It'd been fun to dress up, but she felt so much more herself in her favorite pair of jeans and knit sweater.

Too bad it wouldn't be as easy to switch gears after the earlier conversation with Gabe.

As soon as she stepped outside the women's bathroom, Gabe jogged over to her. "I just heard the news. Someone has tried to break into the clinic."

Chapter Twelve

As they entered the animal clinic, Paige ran up and gave Reg a hug. "I'm so glad you're okay. We heard about the security alarm going off, and I was so worried."

Reg patted her back. "I'm fine. Loki and Lucy, too. You didn't need to rush over here from the reception. Our police department has everything in hand." He motioned to where Detective Paris was speaking with another officer. A man sat on the floor in handcuffs, his back up against a wall.

"Is that the guy who tried to break in? What happened?"

"Yep, that's him. After all the trouble you've been having, I made sure the back door was locked."

Paige nodded her understanding. The back door led to the dumpster and a fenced-in area of yard. They normally kept it locked during the day unless someone had a reason to go out there.

Reg grinned as he continued. "I suppose he thought it would be a good idea to force it open with a crowbar and come in that way anyway. But as soon as the door opened, the chime sounded, and I knew what was going on. I had my shotgun with me, and I guess he didn't expect that from an old doctor."

"Gabe said the security alarm went off."

"Oh, I set that off with the panic button. I didn't want to risk taking my attention off the guy to make a phone call. Figured that would work just as well. And one of the officers was out in the parking lot, so there was backup almost immediately."

"Nicely done." Paige chuckled at the mental image of Reg holding the crook by gunpoint until the police arrived. "Any idea why he tried to break in?"

"I'd like to know that myself, but he's not talking." All humor fled from his face. "Hasn't said a single word. And I heard one of the officers say he doesn't even have identification on him. Which is pretty odd, if you ask me."

She nodded as she stared at the man.

Gabe joined the other officers, casting a firm look at the man on the floor.

That's when the suspect raised his head and made eye contact with Paige. She immediately knew it was the man who'd attacked her in the parking lot. It wasn't only the light blue eyes, but the flash of recognition on his face that faded away an instant later. As though nothing happened, he let his chin drop again to stare at the floor.

Paige shivered. As soon as she could catch Gabe's eye, she waved him over. There must have been something in her expression because his own grew serious as he approached.

"Are you okay?"

She angled herself so that Gabe stood between her and the suspect on the floor. "That's the guy who attacked me in the parking lot."

Gabe didn't seem surprised by her words. He lowered his voice. "So this guy comes after you, follows you to your house, tries to see inside, then shoots at you and runs you off the road. But *tonight*, he tries to break into the clinic."

"Did he think I was here? Or..."

"Was he after the dog?" They both asked simultaneously.

The idea sounded insane, but it was the only thing that made any sense.

Gabe glanced at the suspect. "Which begs the question: why?" He waved Detective Paris over and relayed what Paige said about the guy, and their guess about the dog. "I'd like to be there when you question him if you don't mind. Even if it's just from the other side of the mirror."

"Done. We're going to wrap up a couple things here and then take him in, if you want to join us at the station. I'll wait until you get there to start the questioning."

A deep chuckle drew their attention to the suspect. He'd gone from looking aloof to sporting an odd expression on his face. Paige wasn't sure if there was more humor or fear there. Either way, his mouth stretched as he grinned, reminding her of a clown face without the paint. She suppressed a shudder.

Detective Paris glared at him. "I highly recommend you save it for your statement at the precinct."

That only made the man laugh louder. And then the humor ebbed, replaced by the earlier stony silence as he stared at the floor again.

Yep, the guy was as creepy without his balaclava as he was with it.

Gabe reached over and squeezed Paige's hand briefly before returning his attention to Detective Paris. "That sounds good. I'm going to take Paige and the dog back to her place, then I'll head right over."

"I'll see you there."

Gabe put a gentle hand against Paige's back and directed her away from the suspect as though he didn't want her to have to deal with the guy anymore. "Let's find the dogs and get you home."

His thoughtfulness warmed her heart, but it also made her immediately think of the dance they'd shared earlier. Paige still couldn't believe that she'd admitted she'd been in love with him back in high school.

Seriously, she'd kept the secret for eleven years. Why couldn't she have done so for even one more night?

And then, when Gabe asked her how she felt now, she'd run off to avoid having to answer. She had to put some physical distance between them because apparently, being at her best friend's wedding and in Gabe's arms was a terrible combination.

Now that their emotions from years past were out in the open, Paige seriously doubted Gabe was going to simply let things rest. He was determined. Dedicated.

It was one of the many reasons why she lov—

Ugh!

The guy who had been stalking her and who had threatened her life the day before was finally in handcuffs. She was relieved—really, she was. So why couldn't she relax now that she and Gabe were about to be alone again?

The drive from the animal hospital to Paige's house was way too quiet. Even the dogs were both asleep in the kennel behind the cab of Gabe's Tahoe. He glanced at his passenger, half expecting to find her asleep as well. He wouldn't have blamed her. Goodness knew he was exhausted between the wedding and the excitement at the vet clinic. But she was wide awake and watching everything as it passed by the window.

Now that they had captured the creep who'd been trying to hurt her, there was no more need for Gabe to stay at her house.

He battled the twinge of disappointment. He and Paige had agreed to meet once a week for breakfast. But after the conversation during the dance, he worried she may change her mind. The thought of going back to seeing her irregularly didn't sit well with him at all.

"Are you hungry? We can hit a drive through before we get to your house."

"No, I'm good. I think there's still some fried chicken in the fridge." She glanced at him. "Thanks, though."

At least the tone of her voice sounded somewhat normal.

Something white drifted through the air and landed on the windshield followed by several more. Gabe nudged her arm with his. "Look. It's snowing."

By the time he got them the rest of the way to her house, the few snowflakes had turned into a flurry of white that the windshield wipers had a difficult time sweeping away fast enough.

"This is insane." Paige shook her head, then pulled her phone out and touched the weather app. "I guess it's coming in just as expected, but it looks like it's hitting harder than they thought it would. We've got a winter storm warning in effect. Up to six inches of snow and plenty of ice."

"I hope Megan and Bryce are safely on their way to

warmer weather." He had their flight information on his phone. Once he had the chance, he'd check it and make sure their plane took off okay.

"Me, too."

Gabe's phone dinged. A text popped up from Arnold telling him they were already getting weather-related calls, and that he'd see him at the station. He showed it to Paige. "Here we go again. We should've stowed away on Bryce and Megan's plane. The beach is sounding pretty good right now." He parked his Tahoe in Paige's driveway. "You go unlock the door, and I'll get Lucy out and bring her with me."

Paige nodded her agreement and dashed through the falling snow toward her front door.

He helped lift Lucy from the kennel and set her on the ground, her leash in his hand.

"I'll be back in a few minutes, boy." He patted Loki on the head before closing the door again. He went inside and turned to Paige. "I should probably grab my things and get going before it gets much worse."

Paige nodded, but there were hints of sadness and worry in her eyes.

He gathered the sleeping bag, his duffel bag, and anything else he'd brought and stacked them next to the front door. Paige surprised him with several pieces of fried chicken in a plastic container.

"Thank you." He balanced it on top of his duffel bag.

"No, Gabe. Thank you. For going out of your way to make sure I was safe. For staying with me."

He reached out and lightly touched her arm where the outline of the bandage could be seen through the sleeve of her shirt. "I'm glad it's over. That things can return to normal for you." Lucy whined then and tilted her head in their direction. "You know, normal plus a dog, anyway."

"Yeah, but it's going to be a good kind of different." Paige reached down and rubbed the area beneath Lucy's chin.

Gabe hesitated. It'd been a long day, and he knew Paige was exhausted. But something in his gut said that it would be a huge mistake if he let their conversation from the wedding go unfinished. "Look, Paige. About what was said at the dance…"

She immediately crossed her arms in front of her. "I'm not sure tonight's a good time."

"There's never a good time. We confessed something eleven years after the fact. If that doesn't tell you how easy it is to let time slip through our fingers, I don't know what will."

Her gaze darted to the floor and then the door behind him as she took in a slow, shaky breath.

He waited for her to focus on him again, and his heart clenched at the wary look on her face. Gabe couldn't walk away tonight without knowing how she felt. "This last week has been one of the scariest times in my life. The thought of losing you is excruciatingly painful. But even then, I don't regret a single moment I spent with you. And that includes having to spend the night on that torture device you call a couch."

Paige pressed her hand against her mouth to hide a smile. She shook her head as the humor faded. "Why does this have to be so hard?"

Her words made Gabe's chest ache. "Come here." He drew her into his arms, offering a hug that he needed as badly as she did. "I get it. These last few days have been horrible. I couldn't stand the thought of not being right by your side, because if something were to happen to you, and I wasn't there to protect you…" The words fell away as emotion clogged his throat. He leaned back and studied her face. "To me, what we have here is worth the risk. *You* are worth the risk."

Paige stilled in his arms. She took in a breath. Then another. She rocked to her tiptoes and brushed her lips against his.

He wrapped an arm around her and pulled her closer. When her hand cupped the back of his neck, he kissed her again, pouring into it all the love and emotion he'd kept bottled up. As though he'd finally found the missing piece to a puzzle that he'd waited years to complete.

His radio crackled, then announced a callout nearby.

He broke the kiss, then touched his lips to hers again briefly. She leaned forward, putting her forehead against his chest before raising her head to look at him.

"I wish you didn't have to go back out in this weather."

"Me, too." He wanted to stay, to kiss her again and see what this meant for them. But he'd waited years for that kiss. If he had to, he could wait until tomorrow for another one.

"You'll be careful tonight?"

"I will. And I'll call when my shift is over and I'm home again." He ran his thumb across her chin.

"No matter what time it is."

"I promise."

The small snowflakes turned to huge, fluffy ones by the time Gabe arrived at the police department. The whole parking lot was already dusted as he and Loki made their way inside.

"We've got a problem."

Those weren't the words Gabe hoped to hear, especially coming from Paris. "What's going on?"

"Our suspect was found dead in his holding cell."

Gabe stopped short. "What? How?"

"It looks like some type of poison. We're waiting on toxicology to get the specifics. But by the time he was found, he'd collapsed and wasn't breathing. Attempts to resuscitate him failed." Paris looked as surprised as Gabe felt.

"Did he have something on him that we missed? Something he took once he was alone?"

"It's possible. He still refused to say a word even after we secured him in his cell. No request for a phone call. No demand for a lawyer. No telling us we got the wrong guy. Nothing." Paris shook his head. "It was just plain odd."

Gabe had to agree. "So let's assume he did take something to end his life. Was he afraid he might cave when he was questioned? Or was he afraid that, if he did say something, someone might do far worse to him later?"

"Or was he protecting someone else?" Paris led the way to one of the conference rooms where several people were in attendance, including the chief. Everyone took a seat.

"What's our status?" Arnold asked as he looked around the room.

"We're running facial recognition now," Blake reported. "If our guy is in the system, we'll hopefully get his ID here soon. The lab is running a toxicology screen on him, too, so we'll know what killed him."

Officer Durant held up a finger. "We located a car near the animal clinic. The hood was still warm, but it was parked on the side of the road just out of view behind a series of hedges. We think it was probably his car." She checked her notes. "It does match the description of the vehicle that Paige Wade originally described after someone followed her home from the clinic. We also checked, and his shoe size is consistent with the prints outside of her home. But none of it is definite."

Gabe was certain he was the same man who had been after Paige since the beginning. "Once we get an ID, hopefully we can make a connection between him and Finch." There were still enough unanswered questions to make him uneasy. The guy who had been bothering Paige was dead. But Gabe was the type of guy that liked to have everything wrapped up in a neat little package.

A ping sounded from somewhere in the room and everyone glanced at their phones or smart watches.

"Ah, here we go," Paris announced as he scanned the information on his iPad and then connected to the large monitor in the conference room so that everyone else could see what he was looking at. "We've got an ID. Meet Martin Laramie." A mug shot appeared, and the man looked as animated in it as he had in their custody. "He's got a rap sheet a mile long with everything from assault and battery to robbery to drug possession. It looks like he managed to get plea deals and then got out early on parole."

Gabe read the details as Paris cycled through several screen's worth of information. It angered him that guys like this kept getting out of jail where they could continue down the path they obviously had no intention of veering away from. Well, if Laramie were still alive, Gabe would make sure that attempted murder was added to his list of charges.

A woman popped her head into the conference room. "Sorry for the interruption, but I was told you needed this right away. It's the toxicology report on your deceased suspect." With that, she handed it over to Arnold and took her leave.

Arnold took one look at the result and let the report drop to the table. "Cyanide, taken orally. It would have done the job quick." He frowned, the lines between his brows deepening. He focused his attention on Paris. "See if you can find that connection between Finch and Laramie. There's got to be one somewhere."

"I'm way ahead of you, Chief. Check this out. They were both serving time in the same jail for about six months before Finch was released. Although I don't see any record here of any direct interaction between the two."

"That doesn't mean much, though," Gabe said. "Only that there weren't any issues between them worth putting in the files. If Finch was the go-between, then that means there may be one more person in play here. At least one."

Arnold put his hands on the table and stood. "I'll assign Krautscheid to keep an eye on Paige's place." He gave Gabe a nod. "In the meantime, it's getting late, and we have quite the winter storm brewing, which means these roads are going to be a mess. We're going to have more calls tonight than we'd like. I'm going to need the rest of you on board handling them as best you can. And remember, the most important thing is to be careful out there. Snow doesn't care who's driving the vehicle."

"Yes, sir," echoed around the room as everyone stood and took their leave.

Gabe appreciated the chief still taking precautions with Paige's safety.

He didn't look forward to getting out in the weather, but he was more than prepared with winter gear and hot coffee. Not only that, but he had a call to Paige to look forward to when his shift was over.

The thought of her, at home warm and safe, brought a brief smile to his face.

Even still, he couldn't shake the sense that something was going to happen tonight. Before setting out on patrol, he said a prayer, asking for protection not only for himself, but for all his brothers and sisters on the force.

Chapter Thirteen

Gabe steered his Tahoe through the falling snow. He could still discern where the edge of the road met the shoulder, but that probably wouldn't be true for much longer. They'd predicted up to six inches of snow, and if it continued to fall like this, Gabe was convinced they were going to get at least that. Hopefully, tomorrow most people would stay home if they could.

He'd helped numerous stranded motorists over the last hour. Most were either going too fast for the weather or had run into a ditch or something similar due to the terrible visibility. No one had been injured, which was a blessing.

So far, Loki's assistance hadn't been needed, and Gabe had left him inside the heated Tahoe. He had the heater blasting at floor level to keep his own feet warm. Thank goodness he'd worn two pairs of socks.

Right now, he was responding to a report of a stranded car on the edge of town that someone had called in. This particular highway was barely within Destiny's city limits. Gabe had already been in the vicinity after the previous call.

Not for the first time tonight, the Tahoe's tires hit an invisible patch of ice. Gabe breathed a prayer of thanks for a vehicle that had four-wheel drive.

Something caught his eye up ahead. Gabe squinted through the sea of fallen snow and could barely distinguish the outline of a white vehicle pulled over on the side of the road. If it weren't for the flashers, he wouldn't have seen it at all. It was an extremely hazardous location to be stuck in. The sooner he could help the driver move his car, the safer that driver would be.

Gabe flipped on his emergency lights to announce himself and make his own vehicle more visible as he pulled over behind the white car.

A man stood up from behind the car, a tire iron in his hand. What a terrible time to have a flat.

Gabe called it in to dispatch, reporting his location as well as the situation, before stepping out of his vehicle. "Good evening!" he called out as he approached the vehicle. "I'm Officer Gabe Harrison. You having some trouble?"

"Good evening, Officer. Yeah, I hit something and busted a tire. Good thing I had a spare in the trunk." The man ran a hand over his sparse beard. The heavy coat he wore looked huge on his lanky form. "I appreciate you stopping, but I'm nearly done here. I should be back on the road momentarily." He lifted the tire iron for emphasis.

Gabe motioned to the sky. "It's only supposed to get colder, and this has to be one of the worst places to be stuck. Visibility here isn't great even during decent weather. Why don't I give you a hand, and we'll get you back on the road even faster?"

Instead of looking relieved to have some help, or even annoyed if he'd truly wanted to do this alone, a flash of panic crossed the man's face. A warning bell went off in Gabe's gut.

"The temperature is dropping fast, and I ran into several icy patches in the last half hour." Gabe paused. "Why don't I go get you a bottle of water and a hot pack? It's the least I can do." He didn't wait for the guy to agree. With one eye on the man, he went back to his vehicle.

Gabe put the license plate into his computer. While it searched for registration information, he stuffed a water bottle and a hot pack into one of his pockets.

The results of the search came onscreen. The vehicle was registered to a Catherine Donaldson. No outstanding warrants or tickets.

Well, this clearly wasn't Catherine Donaldson. But it could easily be a relative or boyfriend. He opened the door behind the driver's side and reached for Loki's leash. "Come on, boy."

The German shepherd leapt effortlessly from the Tahoe and watched Gabe expectantly.

"Heel," Gabe instructed. He didn't have to look to know his partner was following directions.

The man skirted around his car until he was between it and Gabe. "No, really. I've got everything handled."

Gabe noticed the lack of a warm hat on the man's head. His hands were bare, too. The man moved again, catching the light emanating from the Tahoe's headlights. That's when Gabe zeroed in on what looked like blood on the handle of the tire iron as well as the man's hand.

"Are you injured?"

The man's eyes widened then. He glanced down at his hands, dropped the tire iron as though it were suddenly red hot, and reached behind his back for something that Gabe could only assume was a weapon.

The moment the gun was visible, Loki raced forward, his long legs making quick work of the distance between them. In a heartbeat, Gabe had his handgun out and squeezed the trigger just as the man fired his own weapon.

The perpetrator took a bullet to the shoulder, knocking him backwards into the snowbank.

As though he'd hit an invisible wall, Loki dropped right where he was. There was no whimper or groan. Simply silence.

"No, no, no!" Gabe kept his weapon trained on the man who was now lying on the ground, blood from his wound a stark contrast to the white powder beneath him. An indentation revealed where he'd dropped the gun. It was easy to see the man was still alive. His breath created thin clouds in the freezing air around them.

Gabe looked to Loki's still form, his heart pounding as rage coursed through him. As much as he wanted to check on his partner, it would do neither of them any good if this guy came to. Instead, Gabe confiscated the gun, rolled the guy over, and secured him with a pair of handcuffs. As soon as he'd made sure there was no one else in the car, Gabe ran to Loki and fell to his knees in the snow.

"Come on, buddy." He ran a hand down his partner's side, the soft fur gliding against his palm. Loki's chest rose once. Twice. "Okay. You're going to be okay." Gabe lovingly petted the dog's head then noticed those brown eyes turn to look at him.

Loki was alive. And awake. Anger washed over Gabe as he thought about what kind of pain his friend must be experiencing. He had to act fast, though. No telling what kind of condition Loki was in. He grabbed his radio. After announcing his call sign, he reported the situation. "Are

143

there any units in the area? I need to get Loki to the vet ASAP."

The radio crackled before Baker's voice sounded. "I'm less than two minutes out, Gabe. Hang in there."

Another officer announced he was on the way.

It killed Gabe to have to stay there and keep an eye on the prisoner instead of running to his Tahoe for the emergency medical kit he kept fully stocked for Loki. He pulled his coat off, keeping his gun trained on the man who remained unconscious in the snow.

He knelt next to Loki, alarmed at the red blood that now stained the snow beneath him. Gabe swallowed hard. "I've got you, buddy." There was a bullet wound that he could see, and judging by the amount of blood seeping into the snow below Loki, Gabe guessed the bullet had exited the dog's body. He pressed his coat against the wound and cringed when his partner whined with pain.

Sirens finally pierced the air. As soon as Baker arrived on the scene and took charge of the prisoner, Gabe whipped his cell phone out and dialed Paige's number. She answered after the second ring.

"Hey, Gabe. This weather is crazy—"

"Loki's been shot. I'm heading to the clinic."

Shuffling sounded in the background. "I'm on my way."

"Paige, the roads are nasty. Be careful."

"I will. I'll meet you there."

The call ended, and Gabe stuffed the phone back into his pocket. He hit the button on his belt that caused the kennel door to open automatically, then he scooped Loki into his arms and stumbled to his feet as a second police car pulled onto the scene.

"Blake!"

The other officer had secured the prisoner in the back of

his police car. He motioned to the new officer, gave some directions, then jogged toward Gabe's Tahoe. "Get in with Loki."

Gabe set Loki onto the floor of the kennel as carefully as he could, retrieved the first aid kit from the back, and then got in with him. His door barely closed before Blake had the Tahoe moving allowing Gabe to focus his attention on Loki. "I need the cab light, Blake."

"Got it!"

Please, God, give Loki the strength he needs to survive this.

As light flooded the kennel, Gabe spotted both injuries that the bullet left behind. He dug in the first aid kit to retrieve gauze that he pressed against the first one. Loki groaned, his body trembling with pain. "I'm sorry, buddy." Gabe took the muzzle attached to the kit and slipped it over Loki's snout and face before fastening it in place.

As much as he hated to do it, he knew it was for his safety as well as Loki's. Gabe could only imagine how much pain his buddy was in. Any attempts to snip or bite at Gabe would be unintentional, but Gabe needed to be able to tend to the wound without worrying about that.

He went back to pressing the gauze against the wounds. He had to stop the blood flow, especially since this weather meant the trip to the hospital was likely going to take longer than it normally would.

"How's he looking?" Blake kept them moving forward.

"It's a through-and-through. I don't think the bullet hit any organs, but he's bleeding heavily."

"We're about five minutes out now."

Gabe appreciated the update. He wanted to pass it along to Paige, to let her know when they'd be there, but he didn't want to take the pressure off Loki's wounds. He said a silent prayer that she'd get to the animal hospital safely in this nasty weather.

When the gauze became saturated, he lifted his hand enough to slap another piece on top and continued to apply constant pressure.

Loki was still awake, but his response to the pain seemed to be lessening, which concerned Gabe even more. "You're a good boy. Such a good boy. You probably saved my life there, buddy. I'm never going to forget that." He refused to think about any outcome that didn't have Loki walking away in one piece.

Paige swiped her sleeve across the window of the clinic for the third time to clear the fog that kept obscuring her view. With the amount of snow falling, she couldn't even make out where the sidewalk ended, and the parking lot began. Hopefully, she'd be able to see Gabe's headlights when he arrived.

As soon as she'd spoken with Gabe earlier, she'd gotten Lucy into the car and then called Selena. Since the tech was only a block away from the clinic, it made sense to swing by and pick her up. While Paige might be able to perform any surgery Loki needed, it would be much easier and more efficient with Selena's help. Especially if they ran into trouble.

Right now, Lucy was in one of the exam rooms with food, water, and toys while Selena prepared the surgical room for Loki's arrival.

"Come on, guys, where are you?" Her breath only fogged the window again. She swiped at it impatiently.

She'd worried plenty about Gabe ever since he left her house earlier. But most of that worrying had been over him getting stranded somewhere, skidding off the road in his vehicle, or getting hit by another vehicle due to bad visibility. What kind of situation had Gabe run into where Loki had been shot? Had Gabe been hurt, too?

The thought had her stomach twisted in knots. This right here was exactly why she'd avoided getting into a relationship with him.

Except she was fooling herself if she thought she'd be less worried right now if they *hadn't* kissed earlier.

"Please help them to get here safely," she prayed.

She glanced at the framed stretcher at her feet and went through her mental list to make sure they were as ready as they could be. It would help to know for sure how bad Loki's injuries were.

Paige registered the ticking of the wall clock. Usually, it was much too loud in the waiting area to hear it. Right now, though, it sounded off every long second that passed.

Finally, a pair of headlights came into view. She recognized Gabe's Tahoe as he drove it up over where the curb would've been and stopped as close to the front doors of the clinic as he could possibly get. "They're here!" she yelled for Selena.

The tech's rapid footsteps announced her approach. Together, they lifted the stretcher and pushed the doors open, locking them in place.

She recognized Officer Blake as he opened the kennel door and waved her over. She peered inside to find Gabe putting pressure on Loki's wounds.

"He's still conscious, but he's obviously hurting." There was no missing the fear that laced his words.

"Gabe? Are *you* okay?"

He blinked at her in surprise, then his gaze softened. "I wasn't hurt."

Paige breathed a silent prayer of thanks. "Alright, let me in there so I can take a look at him."

He quickly shifted positions and backed out of the vehicle, allowing Paige to get inside and assess Loki's condition. Gabe was right, there was significant blood loss. There was also no missing the glaze of pain in the poor dog's eyes. "We need to get him inside now," she called to Selena over her shoulder.

Together, they lifted the dog's eighty-five-pound frame and lowered it as carefully as they could. Paige strapped him into place, noting the amount of blood that had pooled on the floor of the kennel.

Amazingly, Loki's eyes remained open. He blinked at her a moment before turning his attention back to Gabe.

The dog was devoted to his partner. Despite the pain and fear Loki had to be experiencing, the trust was still there even now.

Gabe would be devastated if anything happened to Loki.

Paige swallowed hard. Snow was beginning to cover Loki's fur as Paige continued to hold pressure on the wounds while Blake and Gabe carried the stretcher.

Selena rushed ahead to the surgical room.

"X-ray!" Paige called ahead.

"Already there, Doctor Wade."

Paige was relieved to see that Selena had placed thermal pads on the x-ray table and then covered them with towels. "Let's get him on the table."

Chapter Fourteen

"We need to get him stabilized first," Paige announced as she and Selena worked on Loki. All the while, Gabe hovered nearby with one hand always on his partner. Loki's gaze never left him, either.

She brushed past Gabe as she maneuvered around to get a better look at the wounds.

"Do you need me to move out of the way?" Gabe asked.

Paige shook her head and ran a hand over the dog's shoulder. "I need you to stay right there until I get Loki under anesthesia. The less stress we put on him and the less he moves the better. That means he needs to see you."

Gabe continued to stroke the dog's nose through the gaps in the muzzle. "You're a good boy, Loki."

"Selena, start an IV please. We need to get antibiotics, pain management, and fluids going."

"I'm on it."

The power flickered. Paige thought it was going to stay on, but a moment later, the lights winked out, bathing them in darkness. "The generator should kick on in a few seconds," she said.

As though on cue, the lights came back on.

Paige looked up and met Gabe's eyes. "As soon as we get him stabilized, we'll take some x-rays to see what kind of damage we're looking at. The good news is that the bleeding is under control. His temperature is coming up, too." She reached over and squeezed his hand.

Gabe nodded. "Good. That's good." He watched as Selena got the IV placed and different bags were hung nearby.

"There we go." Paige pointed to the monitors. "His heart rate is coming down, and his breathing is slowing to a more normal rate. That means the pain medication is kicking in." She paused long enough to look Loki in the eyes and rub his ear. "I'm going to give him anesthesia through his IV so we can get some x-rays."

It wasn't long before Loki's eyes drifted closed. As soon as they did, Paige gently removed the muzzle.

Only then did Gabe visibly relax. He stepped back so that Paige and Selena could move Loki as needed.

Paige studied the results. "Excellent." She motioned Gabe over and pointed to the x-ray. "The bullet entered in the hollow area of his right shoulder, passed through tissue, and emerged at the edge of the latissimus muscle. Thankfully, there has been no damage to the bone, which is what we were hoping for."

"So he's going to be okay?"

"I still need to get in there, tie off the bleeders, stitch muscle back together, and clean everything out. Complications can happen. But yeah, given the circumstances, this could have been much worse." Paige put a hand on his arm. "Why don't you go out, check in with the chief, and

I'll let you know when we're done. It could take us a while."

Gabe bent over his furry companion, placed a kiss against the fur between Loki's eyes, and whispered. "You've got this. I'll see you soon."

"I'll take care of him, Gabe. I'm going to do absolutely everything I can, I promise."

Gabe drew her into a tight hug. "I know you will. Thank you," he whispered near her ear.

Reluctantly, he left them in the surgical room and made his way to the waiting area where Blake was seated. "Hey, I had no idea you were still here." Gabe walked forward and shook the man's hand. "Thank you for doing your part in getting us here so quickly. Loki is going into surgery soon, but for right now, he's stable and holding his own."

"I'm real glad to hear it," Blake said and stood.

"Have you heard what the deal was with the shooter? There was blood on his hands, but I didn't see anyone else out there." Gabe wasn't sure if he'd turned his radio down earlier, or if he'd tuned it out.

"He shot a guy who was filling up his car at a gas station. Stuffed him in the trunk then stole the vehicle. They're still trying to figure out if he was running from something, needed some wheels, or what. Anyway, he didn't anticipate getting a flat tire on his way out of town. Couldn't call for help. Obviously, couldn't just hoof it out in this nasty weather. So he had to use the tire iron to change it..."

"...which was covered in his victim's blood," Gabe finished. "Gotta love irony."

"Especially when it leads to saving someone's life."

Gabe's eyes widened. "The victim was still alive?"

"Yep. He's been transported to the hospital." Blake clapped him on the shoulder. "If you hadn't stopped when you did, things might have ended differently for that man."

"I'm glad. Real glad." He said a silent prayer of thanks. "And the guy I shot?"

"He'll live, too." His radio crackled with dispatch asking Blake for an update on his location.

Gabe nodded toward the door. "Was someone able to bring your patrol car by?"

"Not too long after we got here."

"Then go, they need you out there. I'm good."

Blake let dispatch know he was available again. "The chief said to tell you that you and Loki are in his prayers. I think Krautscheid said he'll be by to check on you, too. Call me when Loki gets out of surgery, will you?"

"You got it. Thanks again, man." Gabe watched Blake leave the clinic, a burst of cold air forcing it's way inside along with a flurry of large snowflakes. The doors closed again, and Gabe heard the click of the lock.

He checked his phone then, responding to texts from his fellow officers expressing their concern for Loki, letting him know they were praying, and telling him to let them know if he needed anything.

Unfortunately, going through messages didn't take nearly long enough. Soon he was struggling to find a way to occupy his mind while waiting for news from Paige.

Gabe had spent plenty of time pacing the hallways of hospitals while he waited for a surgery to finish or for word of someone's condition. If not for a friend or family member, it was for one of his fellow officers. Regardless, the air of uncertainty was oppressive.

He could now say that waiting for word on his canine partner was no different. Gabe kept replaying the routine stop in his mind but knew there wasn't anything he could've done differently. Loki was trained to protect his handler, and that's exactly what he did. At least his actions had not only saved Gabe, but the man in the trunk as well.

It was nearly eleven at night, and the snow was still coming down. Loki had been under for over an hour. Gabe had nearly convinced himself to go back into the surgical room to check on him when Paige came out.

She was using a towel to dry her hands off, which she set down on the reception counter. "Everything went as well as I'd hoped."

"He's going to be okay?" Gabe was almost too afraid to ask.

Paige smiled. "Barring infection, I don't see why Loki won't make a full recovery."

The vice gripping Gabe's heart loosened, and a rush of relief coursed through his veins. He whooped and drew Paige into a hug. He lifted her off her feet and spun her around several times before setting her back down. "Praise God. Thank you, Paige. Seriously. I have no idea what I would've done..." Gabe's voice cracked.

Paige was the one to hug him this time. "I know," she whispered. "But he's strong." She stepped away from him, but reached for his hand and led him toward the surgical room. "We got the wound cleaned out, tied off the bleeders, and stitched him back up. I did leave a penrose drain where the bullet went in, and another near the exit wound. That'll help keep the chance of infection down. We'll talk about removing them when the time comes."

She motioned to a large kennel. An IV pump hung on the front of the cage with the lines going through the grates of the cage door. Nearby, Selena recorded something on a clipboard before hanging it on the cage.

There was also a bag of blood hanging there as well. "He needed a transfusion?" Gabe shouldn't have been surprised, not after all the blood Loki lost.

Paige nodded. "We'll need to monitor him every 15 minutes until the transfusion is complete, then keep a close eye on him for a while. He's on some strong pain medication as well as local anesthetic to keep him comfortable. After this kind of physical trauma, it's hard to know how long it'll be before he wakes up."

"I think I'll sit with him for a while." Even if Loki was asleep, Gabe hoped his presence would offer the dog some comfort. With a thankful nod, he accepted a chair that Selena brought in from the waiting room.

"Sounds good. Selena, I'm going to go get Lucy and bring her in here. I'll be right back."

"Okay. I'm going to start the cleanup."

Gabe turned to watch her for a moment. "Hey, Selena. Thanks for everything you did for Loki. I appreciate it."

The young woman smiled. "You're welcome. I'll be praying his recovery is a quick one."

He nodded his thanks.

Moments later, Paige returned with Lucy trotting along beside her. The pittie ran to Gabe, her powerful tail hitting the stool.

"Hey, girl. You look like you're starting to feel better." Gabe rubbed her ears and then scratched her chest. She stared at him, her tongue out and a happy look on her face.

"Her wound is healing nicely," Paige commented as she helped Selena clean. "But I didn't want to leave her at the house alone, especially not knowing how long I was going to be here, or if I'd be able to get back anytime soon with this storm."

Gabe didn't blame her. "I'm glad you did. She's good for moral support." He gave the dog a hug before she moved away from him and started sniffing Loki's crate.

The lights flickered several times before becoming steady again. They listened for a moment to confirm that the generator had turned off. The power must have been restored. Between that, seeing Loki resting as comfortably as possible, and the ebb of adrenaline, Gabe suddenly felt drained. He stifled a yawn.

The next thing he knew, someone was gently shaking his shoulder. It took a second or two to realize he'd fallen asleep. He blinked away the fog and looked up at Paige who was standing over him. "Look," she said with a smile and pointed to the kennel.

Loki was lying in virtually the same spot as he had been before Gabe dozed off. But now his eyes were open.

Gabe was instantly wide awake. "Hey, buddy!" He leaned forward in the chair. "Can I open the kennel door?"

"Of course." Paige opened it for him and moved to the side.

Gabe reached in to gently run his hand over Loki's head. The dog's tail gave a little wag. "That's what I like to see." Another little wag and then Loki licked Gabe's hand. "I love you, too." He pressed a kiss to the dog's nose before looking up at Paige. "This is good, right?"

"Yes, this is good." She beamed at him. "The local anesthetic is still in effect, so he shouldn't be in too much pain right now. He'll be tired for a while, though." She pointed to the blood bag. "His transfusion is complete. Let me get that removed and take his vitals, then you can give him some water."

"When can we take the IV out?"

"Let's make sure he's drinking and eating okay first. I don't want to have to put it back in if he has trouble with either."

"Thank you, Paige." Gabe reached for her hand and kissed it before letting go. He sat up straight and rolled his shoulders, then looked around the room. "Where's Selena?"

"Sleeping. We set up a pallet on the exam table in the other room so she could get some rest."

She removed the blood bag and detached that from the IV. Then she handed a bowl of water to Gabe.

"Is that what you do when you're here overnight?" He placed it on the floor in front of the kennel. Loki promptly struggled to get to his feet and took a long drink. Gabe smiled and patted the dog. "Good boy."

"Yes, but usually I set the pallet up on the x-ray table." She shrugged. "It's a long-standing tradition with veterinarians. It keeps us close to our patients."

Gabe abandoned the chair and eased himself to the floor, his left leg pressed up against the kennel. Loki laid down again and rested his chin across Gabe's knee with a sigh. "You are so tough," Gabe said, his voice soothing. "You saved two lives tonight. You're a hero, Loki." He looked up at Paige. "We don't deserve dogs."

"No, we don't." Paige took the chair he vacated and leaned her elbows on her knees before letting her chin rest in the palm of her hands. "There were a lot of things I was nervous about when you left for your shift. Like the possibility of your vehicle getting stranded somewhere, or the danger of trying to help someone else on a busy road with poor visibility. When you called and told me Loki had been shot..." her voice trailed off, the words she spoke heavy with emotion. "*You* could have been shot."

Tonight was only the second time he'd ever been shot at, and the first time that it was such a close call. None of that mattered, though, because what happened tonight was exactly the type of scenario Paige feared.

He could see the doubt mix with the exhaustion in her eyes, and his own chest tightened in response.

Chapter Fifteen

Paige watched as Gabe gently shifted Loki's head so the dog was completely in the kennel again. Then Gabe turned and crouched in front of her so he could look her in the eyes.

"But I wasn't, Paige. I wasn't hurt." He reached out and took her hands in his. "If it helps, the whole situation scared me, too. When I saw that guy pull his gun, there was a moment there when I wondered if I'd get to see you again." He tapped the top of one of her hands with his thumb. "My next thought was that, if I got shot and survived, you might kill me yourself for scaring you."

She shook her head and smacked him on the shoulder. "That's not funny." She couldn't completely stop the smile that tugged at the corners of her mouth. "And you're not wrong."

"Look, I'm not going to lie and say what I do isn't dangerous. Sometimes it is. But it's the nature of the job, and one I've wanted since I was a kid. All I can do is face every day as prepared as possible, do my job to the best of my abilities, and pray that God will use me to help others." He swallowed hard. "Isn't that all any of us can do?"

The loose bun she'd put her hair in was beginning to fall out. She reached up and removed the hairband, allowing it to flow freely down her back. "Yeah, it is."

"Let's face it. When I considered the possibility of a relationship with the local veterinarian, I had no idea she'd wind up with stab victims on her doorstep." He lifted a hand and twirled a section of her hair around one finger. "Or get shot at driving home from work."

Paige couldn't hold back the chuckle. "You and me both. Thankfully, that's not the norm."

"And thankfully, this isn't the norm for me, either." There was humor in his voice, but the look on his face was serious. He studied her, silently pleading for her to understand.

Her initial instinct was to argue. To tell him it was different. But she knew that wasn't true. She thought about what Megan had said when she came over to watch a movie and how she worried about Bryce, but that being a fire fighter was part of who he was.

The same was true for Gabe. Being a police officer wasn't just part of who he was, it was what he was called to do. She truly couldn't imagine him doing anything else.

He'd been by her side this week, no matter what came their way. As her protector. As her friend. And everything about it had felt right.

The uncertainty in his eyes struck her right to the core. She reached up and gently ran her fingers through his hair.

"Paige. I need you to know that this—you and I—I am all in." He brushed the back of his hand against her cheek. "Are you with me?"

Emotion clogged her throat and had her heart soaring. "I'm with you."

He smiled then. The kind of smile that lit up his eyes as it pushed away all hints of doubt or worry. His hand tangled in her hair as he closed the distance between them with a kiss that felt exactly like coming home.

"Hey guys—" Selena's voice broke in, and they parted to find the tech looking equally interested and embarrassed. "I'm so sorry. I didn't mean to interrupt."

Gabe let his forehead rest against Paige's for a second before standing up, but he reached for her hand and held it. "You're fine, Selena. No reason to apologize."

Selena didn't look convinced, but she shot Paige an amused look.

"Did you get some rest?" The question came from Paige.

"A little."

Lucy went to stand beside Loki's crate. She reached her head in and gently licked Loki's ear.

"It's a good thing the dogs get along, isn't it?" Selena asked, a hint of mischief in her voice.

Paige laughed. "Yes, it is."

Selena reached down to pet both dogs. She fingered Lucy's collar. "Now that you're keeping her, you should get her a tag with her name on it."

Paige had every intention of doing exactly that. She might never know where Lucy came from, but she wanted to make sure the pittie always came back to her.

She looked up to find Gabe studying a brochure he must have picked up from the spares they had stacked on a shelf. This particular one was on the benefits of having your pet microchipped. "Hey, I've got a question for you."

"Oh?" Paige stopped what she was doing and turned. "About what?"

"So I know the chip is implanted into the dog's neck. Each chip has a unique number that is then scanned in and registered. Does it only work with one particular website?"

"No, not necessarily. I mean, the chips themselves are consistent, but there are a lot of different companies that will allow owners to set up an account. Some are free, others offer additional services for a cost. But if the owners don't take the time to register it, then it makes the microchip pointless." Her brows furrowed. "Why do you ask?"

"What does it look like when someone doesn't register the chip?"

"A number comes up on the scanner, but when it hasn't been registered, then no information is associated with it." She paused, her expression shifting from confusion to understanding. "The number we got off her microchip. You think the number could be something else—like the passcode for the SD card."

"The guy we arrested was after Lucy. I know it sounds crazy, but we've gone over her collar and leash and there's nothing hidden in them. It's the only thing that even remotely seems possible. Can you get that number for me? I'll call it in and see if it helps tech at all."

"Sure. I'll be right back." When Paige returned from the front of the clinic, she had a scanner in her hand which she promptly waved over Lucy. A beep sounded and she turned it to show him the number. "There you go."

He pulled a notepad from his pocket and jotted it down.

"Thanks. Let's see if there's anything to this." He pulled his phone out and dialed a number. He brought the phone away from his ear and looked at the screen. "I have zero cell service right now."

Selena checked her phone. "Same here."

Paige followed suit, turning hers around to show him that hers was the same. "Maybe the storm knocked a tower out?"

"It's one thing for the lines to be super busy due to panicked people calling in. But at this time of the night, with the electricity back on, it's not likely." He turned his police radio up and spoke, but only silence greeted him. "Dispatch, do you copy?" Still nothing. "Something's not right."

"What do you mean?" Paige's voice sounded tense even to her own ears.

Selena turned to look at him.

Gabe pocketed his phone, his expression grim. "I think someone is using a signal jammer to prevent us from contacting anyone outside of this clinic."

Paige looked from Selena to Gabe, half expecting someone to tell her this was a joke. She'd only ever heard of signal jammers on TV shows and in movies. "Does that mean what I think it means?"

"The guy we arrested may not have been working alone." Gabe seemed to be thinking through several options. He straightened, his expression tight. "Do you have a land-line up front?"

"Yes! Reg insisted on it."

"Okay, good. Selena, please stay here with the dogs. Close this door behind us and don't open it unless you hear Paige or myself on the other side. Do you understand?"

The tech nodded, her eyes as wide as saucers. "Yes, sir."

Gabe reached for Paige's hand and led her out of the surgical room. The door closed behind them. "I want you to try dialing out—call 9-1-1. Let them know where we are, that I'm here with you, and that we may be under attack.

I'm going to start barricading the back door. Then we'll move to the front."

Paige let go of his hand and went straight to the front desk, her heart pounding against her chest. She picked up the receiver and tried several times to get a dial tone. Nothing.

Fear prickled at the back of her neck and traveled down her spine. She ran to find Gabe pushing a heavy cabinet in front of the back door. "The phone's dead."

He brushed his hands off on his pants and met her eyes. "This will keep anyone from barging in through the back door.

"It's not going to be as easy to fortify the front, though." Paige pictured the glass door and the glass windows that surrounded the waiting room. "Not to mention all the other windows in the clinic. How are we going to keep them from coming in?"

He didn't answer, but the look on his face told Paige everything.

If whoever this was wanted to get into the clinic, they could.

"My Tahoe is right outside. I'm going to grab my rifle, extra ammunition, and any other supplies I can carry. If we're right, we need all the help we can get to defend ourselves."

His words made sense, but the thought of him going out there now, when someone may be lying in wait, petrified her. There was no time to voice her concern because someone pounded on the glass door out front.

Gabe and Paige exchanged a glance. Gabe put one hand on the gun holstered at his side. With his other, he made sure Paige stayed behind him.

As they rounded the corner and entered the waiting

room, Paige breathed a sigh of relief at seeing an officer at the glass door. "Oh, thank goodness. They must have sent someone to check on you and Loki."

She tried to step around Gabe, figuring she should open the door, but Gabe snagged her hand. "Wait," he said, his voice quiet. "Stay back here."

He dropped his hand away from his gun, waved a greeting, and went closer to the door. Only then did Paige notice there were two more men with the officer. They stood several paces back and neither of them was in uniform.

"Hey, Krautscheid. We weren't expecting anyone else out this way until later in the morning." Gabe smiled. It would probably fool anyone else, but Paige could tell it was forced.

"Harrison." The officer gave him a nod. "I was sorry to hear about Loki. I wanted to come by earlier, but this weather has had everyone chasing their tails. How's he doing?"

"He's stable. I'm praying that, with time, he'll make a full recovery."

"That's good to hear. Real good." Krautscheid paused as though waiting for Gabe to say something else. Finally, he motioned to the doors. "If you don't mind, we could use a few minutes indoors to warm up before we get the next callout."

"Hey, could you do me a favor?" Gabe spoke as though Krautscheid hadn't asked him to do something moments before. "We need to get some information back to the chief, but we're having connection problems. I guess the storm knocked out the cell phone tower. I think the battery went out on my radio. Do you think you could relay a message for me?"

Paige watched as the men seemed to size each other up.

Gabe must be testing to see whether the other officer knew about the loss of signal or not. If a signal jammer was being used, that meant Krautscheid's radio wouldn't be working either. And if Krautscheid didn't know about it, then he should be trying his own radio.

Krautscheid tensed, and the two men with him took a subtle step forward, the tension palpable. Paige's stomach clenched, and her heart jumped to her throat.

Wait.

Had Reg put his shotgun back in the cabinet after the guy tried to break in earlier? Or did he take it home with him?

She backed out of the room slowly hoping no one would notice. As soon as she was in the clear, she ran to Reg's office near the back of the building.

Paige's hands shook as she withdrew the keys from her pocket, found the small silver key Reg had given her for emergencies, and inserted it into the locked cabinet. The moment she swung the door open, she breathed a sigh of relief at the sight of the shotgun leaning in the corner. She picked it up and checked the chamber. It was loaded and ready, just as she suspected it would be. She snagged two boxes of shells and raced out of the room.

She approached the waiting room again but stayed out of sight. Stashing the boxes of shotgun shells on a table nearby, she held the gun, pointed down, and listened.

"It's freezing out here. Let me in first, and I'll be happy to contact the chief for you."

Paige couldn't see Krautscheid, but there was no missing the irritation in his voice.

Gabe's hand inched back toward his gun again. "Come on, Paul. I'd like to think we're both way too intelligent for this. Why are you here?"

Something hit the glass then, making Paige jump. It took a second to realize Krautscheid must have smacked the door with his hand or fist. She had to consciously loosen her grip on the shotgun.

"I need the mutt that Finch brought by the clinic the other night. Bring it to me, and we'll walk away."

The moment Gabe saw Krautscheid standing outside the clinic, an almost overwhelming sense of urgency gripped him. If Krautscheid had been here alone, Gabe might have second-guessed his instinct. But the two guys with him weren't police. In fact, he was almost positive that he recognized one of them from a series of arrests last year.

If he was right, then it was one of Warren Teague's guys. Gabe's response warred between disbelief that one of their own could somehow be involved in the drug organization here in town and anger that it might be Krautscheid who was behind the attacks on Paige.

He took several extra heartbeats to respond to Krautscheid's request for Lucy. Enough to keep his focus and shove his emotional responses into the shadows for now.

"I can't do that."

Krautscheid widened his stance and laughed. His eyes grew cold as he stared at Gabe. "I'm not walking away without the mutt."

"Because you need the passcode."

Gabe suspected Krautscheid's involvement, but it was the way the other man straightened his back at the mention of the code that told Gabe he was right. In that case, this move meant Krautscheid was getting desperate.

"What's on the SD card, Paul?"

Krautscheid remained silent.

"I'm willing to bet that this has to do with Teague. What, you in his back pocket? I never figured you to be a dirty cop."

"You have no idea what you're talking about." Except the tension in the other man's voice combined with the flash in his eyes told Gabe he was hitting his mark.

"Come on, Paul. We both know there's no way you're going to let us walk out of here. Let me guess, you'll come in, silence Paige and me, get the passcode off the dog, wipe the security camera footage, then you'll be the one to find our bodies when you supposedly come to check on Loki. Am I close?" Krautscheid didn't respond. "Look, man. We've worked side by side for years. I've always considered you one of my brothers in blue. You owe me the dignity of knowing why I'm dying here today."

Where was Paige? One minute she'd been behind him, and the next she was gone. He hoped she might have retreated to the surgical room with Selena.

Movement to his right caught his attention. Paige stood around the bend from the main waiting area, her back pressed against the wall. A shelf full of dog food kept her hidden from the intruders and offered some protection, but it probably wouldn't for long if they breached the doors and came inside.

She saw him then and lifted the shotgun in her hands. Gabe had no idea if she knew how to shoot it or not, but right now, it didn't matter. That shotgun might make the difference when it came to getting the upper hand.

He gave her a subtle hand motion he hoped she knew meant to wait. She nodded in response.

He focused on Krautscheid. The guy was a good cop

once. Gabe knew that, and he had to bank on the fact that some of that part of him was still buried down deep. The best thing Gabe could do was stall. Someone was going to come by and check on them. The signal jammer also meant Krautscheid couldn't communicate out. If he was still on duty, then his lack of response to dispatch would mean other units would be sent to see if he was in distress.

He had to buy as much time as he could without drawing attention to it. "Finch was in prison at the same time as Laramie. According to records, he had a pretty rough time of it until, suddenly, things got easier. I'm guessing Laramie stepped in and saved his life at some point. Then, once Laramie got out of prison, he eventually called in a favor. Finch really was the go-between, wasn't he?"

Krautscheid's jaw twitched.

The puzzle started to come together. If this was all about Teague, then the only way he was getting out of jail this time was if all the witnesses against him disappeared.

"The SD card has the locations of every witness planning to testify against Teague in the witness protection program, doesn't it?" Teague's men could easily threaten the witnesses to change their stories and kill those who refused.

Krautscheid made a low noise in his throat. "All Finch had to do was pass the card and passcode off to Laramie. But he decided to grow a conscience."

"He was going to turn it in, wasn't he?" Gabe could taste the bile rising in his throat. "And you intercepted the call and agreed to meet him. He thought he was going to hand it over to the police and maybe even gain protection. But you killed him. And then, to add insult to injury, you couldn't find the SD card anyway." Which meant Krautscheid was also the one who cut Lucy. "No wonder Lucy wouldn't come out of Paige's car while you were there. You knew that if you tried to reach for Lucy, she'd take your hand right off as soon as look at you."

"Enough!" Krautscheid's bellow was accompanied by another fist to the glass door. "Harrison, we're coming in. This building is surrounded. There's no way out for you."

"Come on, man. Killing Finch is one thing. Killing a fellow cop…"

"If I don't get that SD card to Teague, I'm a dead man anyway." Krautscheid's eyes were every bit as chilling as the words he spoke.

Gabe watched in horror as Krautscheid took several steps back and motioned for the men with him to proceed. Gabe pulled his gun and jumped behind the check-in counter a heartbeat before the deafening sound of shattering glass filled the air.

Pieces of glass skittered across the floor like an incoming tide. Others glanced off the surface of the counter to land on Gabe's back like hail.

He kept his breathing even as he peered through a narrow space between where one counter ended, and the curved piece began. The two unknown men strode into the waiting room, handguns drawn, and shot several deafening rounds at the counter.

Cold air quickly filled the large area as wind brought in the frigid temperatures outside.

Gabe couldn't see Paige from his location. He prayed she'd stay put and that these guys wouldn't see her, either. He needed to keep their attention on him.

He leaned around the edge of the counter and shot two rounds before ducking back, earning him several shots in return. Wooden splinters flew into the air.

In the background, Gabe registered the sound of dogs barking from the back of the building.

There was no sign of Krautscheid. The coward must be waiting outside so he didn't have to get his hands dirty. The thought of a fellow cop being involved in all of this sent anger surging through Gabe's veins.

He steadied his breathing again. He couldn't allow his emotions to interfere with his focus. He shifted his position and caught a glimpse of Paige. She lifted the shotgun, held it steady against her right shoulder, and looked through the sights.

The men fired again as they inched closer to the counter.

Two more steps, and they'd be able to see Paige.

Two more steps, and Paige would have a clear shot at them.

There!

"Now!" he yelled, and ducked as the boom of the shotgun filled the air. He rose immediately to see that the man closest to Paige was on the ground holding his leg. The other man snarled and turned to face her, his gun raised.

Gabe fired his own weapon, hitting the man square in the chest. He crumpled to the floor, his gun falling from his hand and sliding across the tile.

The first man dragged himself around the corner toward the front door and out of sight. At the same time, more glass shattered down the hall in the vicinity of the examination rooms.

There wasn't much time. He needed to get Paige some-where safer. Gabe skirted around the counter. He picked up the fallen gun and stuffed it into his belt at his back. The man he shot was lying in a pool of his own blood, lifeless eyes staring at the ceiling.

Paige pushed herself away from the wall, the shotgun still in her hands. She handed it to Gabe. "There are more shells there on the table."

He ejected the casing, grabbed another shell, and loaded it. He kept the shotgun trained on the entrance. Like Krautscheid said himself, he had nothing to lose. And a desperate man was a scary one.

"What do you want me to do?" asked Paige. There was no fear in her eyes, only determination.

And Gabe loved her all the more for it.

With no way of knowing how many people were in the building, Gabe knew he couldn't protect Paige from multiple directions. "Get to the surgical room and barricade it from the inside with anything you can. Now!"

Please, God, help us come out of this alive.

Chapter Sixteen

The last thing Paige wanted to do was leave Gabe. But she wasn't about to leave Selena alone in the surgical room, either. This was Gabe's job. She had to trust he knew what he was doing. With one last look at him, she turned and ran through the doorway and right into a man's chest.

He laughed as he grabbed her roughly by the arm. He jammed the muzzle of a gun into her shoulder and pushed her back toward the doorway she'd just come through.

At the same time, Krautscheid entered through the shattered door, his gun trained on Gabe.

"It's over, Harrison. No matter what you do, you can't shoot us both at the same time." He nodded to the guy holding onto Paige. "Take her and don't come back without that passcode. I don't care what you need to do to the dog."

Paige tried to drag her feet as her captor pulled her in the direction of the surgical room, but it had little to no effect. She could hear both dogs barking like crazy on the other side of the door.

The guy positioned her between himself and the door,

the gun pressed into her back. "Open the door. I suggest you get control of the dog, or I'll shoot it."

There was no way Lucy was going to calm down, not based on the barks and snarls inside. All Paige could do was hope that opening the door and letting her out would be enough of a distraction for Paige to get away from her captor.

"Get down, Selena!" she yelled as she yanked the door open.

As Paige expected, Lucy came tearing through the opening, a ball of fur and teeth. She ran right past Paige and her captor, bumping into his leg and throwing him off balance. Paige took advantage of it, ducking down and around him, hoping to get through the door in time to close it again before he realized what was happening.

Instead, Paige was shocked to see Loki pull away from Selena, slide through the door on all four paws, and latch on to the man's gun arm. The gun clattered to the ground as Loki continued to shake it and growl.

"Get it off me!" the man screamed. "Get it off!"

Selena watched with wide eyes. "He was tearing at the kennel and pulled out his IV. I was afraid he was going to rip his stitches, so I opened the door to give him a sedative."

"It's fine," Paige assured her. She grabbed the guy's gun and trained it on the man who had done the same thing to her moments before. "If you move, I will shoot you."

"Okay, okay! Get the dog off me!"

Paige had no idea what command to give to make Loki back off. Other than worrying about Loki hurting himself further, she wasn't in a hurry.

She glanced behind her but couldn't quite see what was going on at the front of the clinic.

"Come on, Gabe. Come on," she whispered. "Please stay safe."

A gunshot pierced the air. Paige instinctually ducked and gripped the gun tighter, her heart lodged in her throat. Was Gabe hurt? *Breathe, Paige.*

One more gunshot, which sent a jolt of fear through her, echoed off the walls.

Silence.

Please, God.

Sirens pierced the air from somewhere outside the clinic.

"Paige! Are you okay?"

She didn't think she'd ever been so glad to hear Gabe's voice in her life.

"I'm okay. Loki has this guy, I've got a gun on him, too."

"Good. Stay right there. We've got help coming."

Paige couldn't see what was going on up front, but she could hear people coming in and voices. A moment later, Gabe came around the corner with Lucy on a leash in one hand.

"Are you hurt?" she asked, scanning him from head to toe, thankful there didn't seem to be any obvious injuries. She breathed a silent prayer of thanks. "The gunshots..."

"No. Honey, I'm good." He handed Lucy's leash to her and then took the gun she was holding. "Krautscheid tried to shoot Lucy. I got him in the shoulder instead." He gave Loki the command to let the man go. "Good boy, Loki. Good boy." Gabe still had to reach down and grab Loki by the collar to encourage him to back off.

Officer Baker came in then and took control of the situation, reaching down to put handcuffs on the man who'd attacked Paige. Officer Durant came into the room with Krautscheid, his arms handcuffed behind his back. He was limping in addition to bleeding from the bullet wound in his shoulder.

Gabe must have seen that she noticed. He grinned. "The leg? That's all Lucy." He called into the surgical room, "We're safe, Selena. Everything is under control."

Selena emerged, and a slow smile brightened her face. She released a huge breath. "Even if you hadn't opened that door, Paige, I don't know that I could have kept those dogs inside."

"They had a job to do," Gabe said. "And they both knew it."

Paige looked down at the pittie who refused to take her eyes off the man who stabbed Finch. She scratched her ear. "Good girl." She scanned Lucy's bandage but didn't see any evidence that she'd further injured herself.

There was no obvious worsening of Loki's wounds, either, but the dog immediately lay down on the floor and began to pant. Selena noticed it, too. "I'm going to get him back in the kennel and see if I can get him to calm down a little." She reached for Lucy's leash. "Here, I'll take her, too." Once Selena got them into the room, she closed the door again.

Detective Paris came in and held out a hand for Gabe to shake and gave Paige an appreciative nod. "I'm glad you're both okay." He glanced at Krautscheid who was being escorted out of the building along with the other man, and a muscle in his neck pulsed. "We got a report of shots fired from a neighbor in this area. When we couldn't get ahold of you, the chief sent patrols over." He paused. "I never would have believed one of our own could've been involved."

"There was a fourth man. He'll have shotgun pellets in his leg."

"Yep, we found him outside. We have him in custody." He grinned. "You two make a good team."

Gabe took out his notebook and tore off the page with Lucy's microchip number written on it. He handed it to Paris. "We believe this is the passcode for the SD card." Gabe told him what was on it. "I don't think anyone gained access to the information. But it does mean there's a leak somewhere."

Paris nodded grimly. "I'll contact WITSEC and make sure the witnesses are moved to new locations as a precaution. I'm going to get this back to the station. This is going to be quite the mess to sort through."

No doubt. Paige cringed when she thought of the kind of cleanup it was going to take to get the clinic back in order. The shattered front door alone...

Her thoughts were interrupted when Gabe stepped in front of her. He cupped her face with both hands. "Are you sure you're okay? What happened here tonight... When that guy had you..." He took a steadying breath. "He's lucky that Loki got to him first."

"I know." She rested her palms against his chest. "Not knowing who fired those shots and whether you were alright. It was horrible." She leaned forward, and he pressed a kiss to her forehead. "I'd like to officially vote that we don't do this again."

"I second that." He kissed her briefly. "I'd better go see if they need any help. We're going to need to give our statements, too."

"I'm good. Go. I'll check on the dogs and make sure they're okay."

He studied her face for a moment before giving a decisive nod. "I'll be back."

Paige knew he would be. She opened the door into the

surgical room and slipped inside. Lucy trotted over, wagging her tail and a happy look on her face. "You are a good girl, Lucy. Good girl." She ran a hand over the dog's sides and examined her face and teeth, finally convinced she was in good health. "How's Loki doing?" she asked as she approached the kennel Selena had put him back in.

"Considering he helped save the day? He's doing remarkably well." Selena made a note on the clipboard and hung it back up. "Obviously, I'm not the doctor, but I'm thinking he should stay here for at least a day or maybe even two before we release him."

"Definitely." Paige lowered herself until her head was level with Loki's. "Thanks for saving my life, buddy."

"He's tough," Selena acknowledged. "So is that cop friend of yours."

Paige turned to see the amusement in the tech's eyes. "Yes, he is."

Selena laughed. "Firmly in the friend zone, huh?"

"Yeah, well, things change." Paige grinned.

The last twelve hours were insanely busy, and Gabe was exhausted. After the events at the animal hospital, he and Paige gave their statements. Then Paige stayed at the clinic to meet up with Reg and start figuring out how to patch up the door and begin the insurance process.

Meanwhile, Gabe had gone to the station with Baker and Durant. There was no way he was going to miss listening in when Krautscheid and the men with him were questioned. It wasn't the same being at the station without his furry partner, but it was best for Loki to stay at the clinic until Paige felt he was well enough to be released.

Paige.

Other than a couple of texts for updates, he hadn't spoken to her since he left the clinic. He pulled up to the curb in front of her house and smiled.

She'd messaged to say that Bryce and Megan were planning to do a video call this morning. They were hoping to hear all about the case and make sure that both Paige and Gabe were okay. Paige invited him over to her house to join in, and he wouldn't have missed it.

All signs of exhaustion faded the moment Paige opened the door and greeted him with a smile. "Hey, you," he said, slipping an arm around her and pulling her in for a hug. "I've missed you."

"I've missed you, too." A tone sounded behind her. She grasped his hand and pulled him over to the couch. "That's them!"

She pressed a button on the laptop sitting on the coffee table. Bryce and Megan appeared, both looking relaxed and happy. They were also both wearing sleeveless shirts and had obviously been out in the sun.

"Oh, my goodness, I'm so jealous of your warm weather," Paige told them. "We got six inches of snow here yesterday." She paused. "You guys look great. Are you having fun?"

"So much fun! The pools here are amazing," Megan stated.

"And the unlimited buffet is the way to go," Bryce added. "Trust me, if you go on a trip like this, splurge for the buffet. It's worth every penny."

Gabe pointed at the camera. "That's what I'm talking about."

They visited for a few minutes until Bryce's expression

grew more serious. "So update us on the case. It's really all over?" He looked at Paige. "Are you okay?"

"It's over." Paige exchanged a glance with Gabe. "And yeah, we had some close calls, but we're okay."

Gabe reached over and briefly squeezed Paige's hand, the motion not visible on screen. He and Paige then filled their friends in on everything that had happened since the wedding.

"So poor Finch really was an unfortunate middle guy?" Megan frowned. "I almost feel bad for him."

"Me, too," Gabe agreed. "Laramie saved his life in prison and as soon as he got released, he came to collect on the debt. Finch was on the straight and narrow, but when you get in with that crowd, saying 'no' isn't an option."

"Did you ever figure out where Lucy came from?" The question came from Megan.

"Oh! I didn't even get a chance to tell you," Gabe said to Paige with a light nudge against her arm. "Paris found out that Finch adopted her from one of the local shelters three days before he died. Apparently, he asked that she be microchipped but never did register it."

"So the microchip was specifically for the number that was later used as the passcode." Bryce shook his head. "It's pretty ingenious."

"Then he must have given that number to whoever supplied the SD card and requested it be the passcode." Paige looked thoughtful and then a little sad. "I guess he adopted her simply to use as a fail-safe when it came to the exchange?"

Gabe could tell she felt bad for Lucy. "I don't know about that. He spent a great deal of money on supplies for Lucy. He may have used her as a fail-safe, but I think he had every intention of keeping her. He risked his life to bring her by the hospital so that you could save hers."

"That's true." A smile replaced the frown on Paige's face.

"We found several suitcases in the trunk of Finch's car," Gabe continued. "We think he was going to hand the SD card over to the police and then disappear completely."

"But Krautscheid got to him first." Bryce's tone was cold.

Megan shook her head. "It's scary how money and drugs can change people like that." She leaned into her husband's side, and he put an arm around her. "Did you guys figure out where the SD card and passcode came from in the first place?"

"Unfortunately not." Gabe knew that Paris was working with WITSEC to figure out who the mole was, but it wasn't going to be easy. "I'm afraid any direct information died along with Finch. There's an open investigation, though, and all witnesses whose names were on that SD card were moved to new secure locations. Warren Teague will be going away for a long time."

Bryce and Megan told them a little more about what they had planned for the day. Bryce looked at his watch. "We have a reservation for dinner so need to go here in a minute. But we are so glad you both are okay. It bothered us to leave while all of this was going on."

"I know, but we're glad you did," Paige said. She glanced at Gabe with a smile. "See, we told you we had it handled."

Megan looked first at Paige and then at Gabe as a slow smile spread across her face. "Are you two...?"

Gabe had hoped he and Paige might have a chance to talk about what was happening between them before saying anything to their friends. But between Megan's grin and the way Bryce raised an eyebrow, that wasn't going to happen.

Offscreen, he rested the back of his hand against Paige's knee. With nearly no hesitation, she placed her hand in his, lacing their fingers together.

He gave her hand a squeeze then lifted them into view of the camera.

Megan squealed. "I knew it!"

Paige rested her forehead against Gabe's arm, her face pink, before looking up with a smile and a shrug. Gabe pressed a kiss to her temple.

"It's about time, you two," Bryce said with a chuckle. "Alright, we need to run. We'll talk to you guys soon."

"And I look forward to hearing all the details," Megan said, pointing a finger at Paige.

The screen went dark, creating a muted reflection of Gabe and Paige where their friends were moments before.

"Well, that went sideways quick, didn't it?" Gabe asked with a chuckle. He looked at their joined hands and rubbed the top of her thumb with his own. "Yesterday was stressful and crazy. I didn't know what you were thinking after everything went down." He shifted to face her. "I couldn't have blamed you if you changed your min—"

"Gabe?"

The sound of his name, barely above a whisper, stopped him midsentence. "Yeah?"

"Kiss me, please."

He leaned in and teased her lips with a brief kiss. "Yes, ma'am," he said, then captured her lips with a kiss as he drew her close.

Epilogue
Four Months Later

Gabe stood beside Bryce and watched as he flipped burgers and brats over burning coals. His stomach growled in anticipation.

On a second grill, corn on the cob cooked along with foil packets of potatoes, bell pepper, and onions. The smell filled Bryce and Megan's backyard as their guests visited with each other.

After an unusually cold winter in general, it was the beginning of March, and the warm Texas sun promised nicer days ahead. Gabe was glad Bryce and Megan waited until now for their barbecue.

Megan walked across the porch and pressed a kiss to her husband's mouth before saying something that had them both laughing. They'd been married nearly four months, and Gabe had never seen them happier.

He scanned the small crowd until he spotted the dark-haired beauty on the other side of the porch. She was leaning against the railing looking out over the backyard. Gabe walked her direction, laughing when he realized what she was watching.

Loki and Lucy were chasing each other around the yard. Loki had a tennis ball in his mouth, and Lucy was determined to get it from him, even though she'd proven that she wasn't a ball dog. If she did manage to get it, she'd quickly lose interest until it was time to chase Loki again.

Paige saw Gabe coming and flashed him a smile. "Hey, you. Dinner about ready?"

"It's getting pretty close." He put his arms around her and nuzzled her ear. "Why, are you hungry?"

"Starving." She turned in his arms to face him. "I love their porch. With the roof over it, Bryce and Megan can spend time out here no matter what the weather is like."

Gabe could easily imagine sitting on a wooden swing with Paige on a porch of their own someday. He'd poke her in the ribs to make her giggle, the motion causing the rhythm of the porch swing to be thrown off. Then he'd kiss her until neither of them even noticed.

"I want this. The house. The porch. The dogs running around in the backyard. Maybe a kid or two eventually." He looked into her eyes. "I want all of that with you."

Her eyes widened a little but then crinkled to match the smile gracing her lips. "I'd like all of that with you, too."

"So if I were to ask you to marry me, what would you say?" He slipped a hand into his pocket and closed his fist around the small ring box he'd been carrying around with him for several days.

"Why don't you ask me and find out?" She reached up and ran her fingers through his hair, sending goosebumps skittering across his scalp.

"I just might have to do that. You know, somewhere romantic. Private. I hear that's what you ladies prefer."

"You've been talking to Megan." Amusement glittered in Paige's eyes.

"It's natural that I'd go to our mutual friends for advice on the matter." He loved it when they teased each other like this. He tugged her close and placed a kiss on her nose. One hand was still in his pocket, and it snagged Paige's attention.

Her eyes widened. "Do you have a ring with you?"

"Maybe. I wanted to have it close in case the perfect moment presented itself."

"It's burning a hole in your pocket, isn't it?" She nibbled on her bottom lip as a smile tugged the corners of her lips upward.

"Yes. Yes, it is." Gabe chuckled. "I'm thinking I should have left it at home and planned the perfect romantic evening instead."

"Well, you're here. I'm here. The ring's here." Paige gave him a cute little shrug. "Besides, you're always so sweet. Anywhere is romantic when I'm with you."

Her words in combination with that shrug made him want to pull her into his arms and kiss her senseless right there on their friends' porch.

Instead, he withdrew the small box from his pocket and opened it. "Paige Wade, I've loved you for about as long as I've known you. I'm convinced God made us for each other. I want nothing more than to spend the rest of my life working together with you to turn the everyday into something extraordinary." He took the ring from the box and held it out to her. "Will you marry me?"

Paige touched the ring with the tip of one finger. "It's beautiful." She looked up at him, a section of hair falling across her cheek. "Yes, Gabe Harrison. I'd love to marry you. *But*," and she emphasized the word with a smile, "I have two conditions."

That got his attention. "And what might they be?"

"First, I want a crazy simple wedding. With the understanding that I might wear jeans and tennis shoes instead of a dress."

Gabe chuckled at that. "Honey, I'm all over a simple wedding. As far as what you wear, all I want is for you to be happy. Besides, if you're wearing jeans, my wearing a suit would be way over the top. So I guess I'd just have to wear jeans, too. You know, so we'd match and all." He leaned in for a quick kiss. "We've got that settled. What is the second condition?"

"I don't want an extended engagement. We've been apart long enough, don't you think?" Her voice softened with the question, her eyes full of hope and love as she waited for his response.

"I'd marry you tomorrow," he said. "You'll get no argument from me." He looked toward the sky and slowly counted off the conditions using his fingers. "So we've got the possibility of wearing jeans to our small, simple wedding after a short engagement." He looked at her then, gently tweaking her chin. "I believe your conditions have been met, my dear. Are you sure that's all you've got?"

Paige laughed. "Yes, I'm sure."

"Because I have ten fingers. You've got room for eight more conditions if you're feeling up to it."

She smacked his chest with her left hand, but he caught it and held it against his heart. "What do you say, Paige?" He lifted the ring and paused at the tip of her ring finger. "You ready to do life with me?"

"Absolutely."

He slipped the ring onto her finger, then captured her lips in a kiss that promised a future together.

Thank you for reading ***Frozen in Jeopardy***. This book was so much fun to write. Be sure to pre-order the next book, ***Beneath the Surface***, to read Detective John Paris and Eve Marks's story!

As the county's chief medical examiner, many of the bodies coming into the morgue hold a mystery that Genevieve "Eve" Marks is determined to solve. In discovering what happened to the victims in her care, she can be their voice when they are no longer able to speak for themselves. Until one particular body includes a message challenging her to examine the past and solve a puzzle before the killer strikes again.

Detective John Paris is leading a murder investigation that's going nowhere. What he desperately needs is a break in the case. Unfortunately, that break comes in the form of another body that is obviously tied to the first. Even more disturbing than the idea that he may have a serial killer on his hands is the fact that the beautiful Eve Marks seems to be a target.

Pre-Order Beneath the Surface Today!

Want a FREE BOOK?
Sign up for Melanie D. Snitker's
newsletter and get ***Fear the Shadows***,
A Danger in Destiny novella, FREE!
This is Chief Arnold Dolman's story
and is exclusive to newsletter members.
Sign up today!

Note from the Author

Thank you so much for reading Gabe and Paige's story. I can safely say that this was one of my favorite books I've ever written. It was so much fun from the characters (both human and canine) to the storyline.

I named Loki after my own dog. We adopted him when he was six months old. He's clearly a mutt, but we were curious and sent in his DNA for analysis. It turns out he's primarily Australian cattle dog followed by German shepherd.

I have a confession: I have never been a dog person. Until Loki, that is. We bonded quickly, and I'm so thankful we found each other.

One of my favorite things about this book was all of the research I got to do.

When I originally reached out to our local police department, Lieutenant Gerald Moran responded. He was awesome about answering my many questions concerning K-9 units and the vehicles they use. He then put me in touch with a K-9 officer who could help me with specifics. I have no doubt this book wouldn't be the same without that information.

I then had the opportunity to go on a ride along with Officer Tim Cox and his K-9 partner, Barco. I learned so much about the interactions between a handler and his dog, how the dog tracks, and was able to ask a ton of questions.

When it came to the medical aspect of Paige working on both Lucy and Loki, I spoke with Dr. Janice Price, one of our local veterinarians, to get advice. Knowing how to approach those scenes made writing them so much easier.

I hope the extra medical and K-9 details made the story and characters all the more enjoyable for you all.

Special Thanks

Beth, I've enjoyed brainstorming together on our latest writing projects. Thanks for your help and suggestions. It's been so much fun, and I'm thankful for your friendship.

Many thanks to Rachel, Mom, Steph, Denny, and Kati for reading early copies of this book. You ladies are all amazing. I appreciate you!

Trish, I so appreciate you taking on my book last minute. Your editing skills are fabulous.

Lt. Moran, I appreciate you taking the time to answer my many questions and for arranging the ride along. All of the information was a huge help.

Dr. Price, thank you so much for going through my medical questions and answering them with such great detail. Your help was invaluable, and I enjoyed our conversations.

Tim, going on the ride along with you and Barco was a wonderful experience. It was an honor to meet you both.

Doug, Xander, and Sydney, thank you for your love and support. I couldn't do this without you!

Most of all, Father, thank you for your faithfulness. I pray that you bless this book and those that read it.

About the Author

Melanie D. Snitker is a *USA Today* bestselling author who writes inspirational romance and romantic suspense. She and her husband live in Texas with their two children. They share their home with three dogs and two terrariums filled with small critters. In her spare time, Melanie enjoys photography, reading, training her dog, playing computer games, and hanging out with family and friends.

https://www.melaniedsnitker.com/

Books by Melanie D. Snitker

Danger in Destiny

Out of the Ashes

Frozen in Jeopardy

Beneath the Surface

Caught in the Crosshairs

Brides of Clearwater

Marrying Mandy

Marrying Raven

Marrying Chrissy

Marrying Bonnie

Marrying Emma

Marrying Noel

Love's Compass Complete Series

Finding Peace

Finding Hope

Finding Courage

Finding Faith

Finding Joy

Finding Grace

Books by Melanie D. Snitker

<u>Love Unexpected Complete Series</u>

Safe In His Arms

Someone to Trust

Starting Anew

<u>Healing Hearts</u>

Calming the Storm

I Still Do

Don't Kiss Me Goodbye

<u>Sage Valley Ranch</u>

Charmed by the Daring Cowboy

<u>Welcome to Romance</u>

Fall Into Romance

A Merry Miracle in Romance